RECENT BORZOI NOVELS

MEEK HERITAGE

MEEK HERITAGE

BY

F. E. SILLANPÄÄ

Translated from the Finnish for the first time by

ALEXANDER MATSON

ALFRED A. KNOPF · NEW YORK

1938

Originally published as
HURSKAS KURJUUS
Kustannusosakeyhtiö Otava, Helsingfors, 1930

MANUFACTURED IN
THE UNITED STATES OF AMERICA

FIRST AMERICAN EDITION

CONTENTS

Prelude	3
Birth and Childhood	9
The Poor Relation	61
Towards Manhood	97
The Heart of Life	125
Death Does its Best	171
The Rebel	209

MEEK HERITAGE

✡

 JUSSI — or Juha or Janne — Toivola — according to the church register Johan Abraham Benjamin's-son — was a repulsive-looking old fellow. During the latter part of his life he was entirely bald except for a fringe of hair, clipped on some unknown past date, that stuck out under his cap over his ears and at his neck. His face, too, was covered with a mongrel growth of tangled hair; only the sharp nose was clearly visible. This was because hair grew round his eyes as well, and as the peak of his cap cast a shadow, one saw in that region of his face only two sunken harsh points of light into which no decent person cared to look.

One meets occasionally with persons whose glance is instinctively avoided, but usually for entirely different reasons than in the case of Jussi Toivola. In his eyes there was nothing awe-inspiring; the expression in them could rather be construed as an attempt at a smile; but there was a hint of insanity in them, and the hardest test to which a man can subject his strength of mind is to look long into the smiling eyes of a lunatic, for their smile seems, in a spirit of fellow-feeling, to be suggesting awareness of what one would not at any price admit existed in oneself. One half expects the demented old woman before one suddenly to say something of the kind aloud for all to hear. . . .

Jussi Toivola, to be sure, was no lunatic; withered though his brain may have been, there was nothing wrong with its balance. The farmers in the locality actually regarded him as a cunning rogue and skilfull agitator. And when it became known that he had been involved during the rebellion in a gross murder, judgment was pronounced on him without further ado. The officer entrusted with the task of cleaning up the district put an end to his life one spring night together with the lives of eight others of his kind.

The effect of the death sentences on the slack local population, which had not foreseen such an eventuality, was on the whole mildly stupefying. Almost, voices tended to tremble whenever the subject cropped up during those first few days. But in Jussi Toivola's last moments there was one minor incident that irresistibly provoked laughter because it was somehow so typical of him. The rebels were shot in a grave dug ready for them in the graveyard, and Jussi chanced to be the last. Whereupon instead of remaining standing he lay down on the pile of corpses — to save trouble, like. Wasn't that Jussi all over? Only he was not shot lying down, but ordered to get on to his feet.

4

" In war one has to *enjoy killing* — if war is not to be a failure," a Finnish warrior of the inkpot has written — the italics are his — apparently with truth.

But war, in an exact sense, is nothing in itself; it is a certain fleeting relationship between individual and collective fates. It passes, but the fates involved are treasures achieved, in which respect they are equal. Very soon after the battles an individual human soul can attain to a moment when the eye no longer, even by an effort of will, halts at the inessential surface, at the physical exertions, the dirt, the hunger and cruelties, but penetrates irresistibly deeper, where all are as though petrified and still in their various attitudes. There no one is nobler or more justified than another, for through the agency of the warring parties circumstances have clashed of which the fighters have no inkling. The dead rise and wonder why they have been buried in this fashion in separate graves; they cannot at all remember what meaning attaches to this discrimination. Jussi Toivola and the officer are old acquaintances; somewhere on a clear night the officer once shot Jussi. It must certainly have happened in a very offhand manner, as he failed entirely at the time to notice how important a man Jussi in reality is. . . .

BIRTH AND CHILDHOOD

Jussi Toivola came of landown-
ing stock, though few among the
present younger generation were
ever aware of this circumstance,
for of what interest were the remote phases of his past to anybody, that they should inquire
about them? Even now there are
highly thought-of kinsmen of his living two or three
parishes away, though Jussi, to be sure, was so thoroughly
estranged from them that he never even thought of them
when his revolutionary activities brought him into peril.

He was born in a certain south-west Finland parish,
on a farm called Nikila in the village of Harjakangas
in the year 1857. His birth took place on a Friday evening before Michaelmas. The atmosphere peculiar to
the eve of that autumn festival was already strong in
the farmhouse and yards that day, mingling with the
strangely cloying atmosphere that seems to radiate from
a woman about to give birth to a child. It had rained
heavily all the morning, but towards evening the sky
cleared and the sun shone on the many-tinted birch and

aspen woods and the revived green of solitary spruce-trees.

The master of Nikila, Benjamin, a drooping man of fifty with a tobacco-stained jaw, came on unsteady feet down the steps leading from the attic to the yard. He was dressed in a soiled burlap blouse, long and gathered in with a leather belt, but the blouse and his shirt were unfastened at the top, leaving a large expanse of bony red chest exposed to the autumn air. Patently a man slowly drifting to ruin; an old farmer in that state, blouse-clad in the farmyard, and a brandy-still bubbling away in a shed, these blended harmoniously with the spirit of the place as revealed in the worn corners and smelly foundations of the house. Benjamin had married thrice and now his third wife was about to give birth to her first child. The cupper-woman, her arms bare and her face sweating, was carrying water to the bath-house. When she saw Benjamin set off towards the village she shouted:

" You stay at home this evening, old man! "

" And you, old hags, keep to your own mangers," Benjamin growled, and strode on in the direction of the village, on his flushed aged face a self-satisfied smile that reflected both the placid daylight without and the equally placid secret thoughts of an old man within.

". . . Women bear children . . . women are like that, always having children . . . this very minute my third wife will be giving birth to a child, but that cupper-woman, she won't have any more . . . eh, eh, eh, boys. . . .

". . . I'm off to Ollila, to see old man Ollila . . . not a bad sort, if he does come from Kokemäki. Drunk as often as I am, shouldn't wonder if he isn't drunk now, and what's to stop him, him with a great strapping boy like the hindquarter of a bear . . . and always plenty of rye. The devil never gets any poorer, even with all that mash . . . I, I've got a third wife already and a child coming again . . . cupper-woman bossing the place, but I'll soon stop women at their games. . . . Feels good to put women in their place . . . every one of my wives has tasted the stick and this one'll get hers soon. . . ."

In Benjamin's veins the spirits he had drunk coursed at their sweetest; his cheeks glowed like bunches of rowan-berries, his eyes sought something near at hand on which he could vent his good humor. He tried to start a quarrel with some potato-pickers and asked Husari's brats:

" Is your father at home? "

" Yes," answered the boy.

" What's he doing there? "

" Don't know."

" He'll be beside your mother," said Benjamin, chuckling with laughter as he turned on to the track leading to Ollila.

The name of this third wife of Benjamin's was Maja. By birth she was a daughter of the very farm he was about to visit; that is to say, she was not this present Kokemäki man's girl; her brother had sold Ollila to him. Having made up his mind to marry into a farm on the other side of Tampere, her brother had no use for their old home and so sold it. That left his sister Maja sitting on a very weak branch indeed. She had a few rubles of her own, but nobody seemed to want them. The feeble attempts she made to bedeck herself and cut a figure only awakened laughter; there was something comical in them, and in the end the community saw to it that they were fittingly punished: Maja gave birth to an illegitimate child. The baby died quickly enough, but by then the rubles were all spent and the only road for Maja was that always open to women. She went into service as a maid. People prophesied new falls from grace for Maja, for she was a weak-willed person. These prophecies, however, were not fulfilled. But when the mistress at Nikila died about Michaelmas and Maja went there that same autumn as maid, people said: " Well, there's Benjamin's next wife." And this time they were right. Maja lay now on the bath-house platform at Nikila with Lovisa, the cupper-woman, fussing in attendance on her.

It was an occasion she had fervently hoped and waited for; her life up to now and especially her mistresshood had been a fumbling and inharmonious affair and it had entered her weak little brain that if she were to present her husband with an heir, that would enable her to get properly started. What had been lacking in her life so far was a proper start, and the lack of that was clearly not her fault. How could she be to blame for the fact that her life had somehow failed to follow the lines

laid down for the lives of farmers' daughters? She had
been in service for five years without feeling her new
status a degradation; it was merely something tem-
porary, carrying on until she got properly started. She
fell in at once with Benjamin's hints to Màja there was
something almost pleasing in the fact that the master
was what he was, old, tobacco-stained about the chin,
fond of drink — and a widower. In feeling this, no idea
of her own lowly state flitted through her mind; it was
only that she felt they were a fitting couple for this particular farm.

That, however, was her mood only during the time
when she knew for certain that she was to become a lawful wife and had a whole week in which to let her fancy
dwell on the announcement next Sunday in church that
" the farmer Benjamin Benjamin's-son, widower, and the
young maiden, the farmer's daughter Maria Josefina
Sefania's-daughter . . ." Only what the parson did an-
nounce was " maidservant on the same farm " — not a
word about any young maiden. And in other respects,
too, Maja was soon to notice that even now she had not
got properly started. Indeed, marriage brought about
hardly any change whatever in her condition. She could
not bring herself to address Benjamin by any other name
than master, and the girls called her Maja as before.
The master, again, used the contemptuous term " old
hags " to convey his feeling for women in general; when
he was in an especially good humor he said " womenfolk."

The same everlasting nameless anxiety that had weighed on Maja while she was hoping to become a wife continued after her marriage. The proper start had always to be postponed. Things ought to have been so-and-so and so-and-so, but it all had to be put off for tomorrow. One modest attempt at asserting herself she made: she was rude to the cupper-woman in the hope that the woman would keep away from the house. But the result was that the master came home one day in a vile temper and shouted: " If you old hags — cows — don't mind your own business, I'll — " Benjamin seemed to draw on the whole force of his alarming old-ness and ugliness and proclaim his superiority to all old hags. Benjamin's life had not suffered from the lack of a proper start; Maja had to respect him. And the cupper-woman on her part showed that she bore no malice; al-most she was more friendly to Maja than before.

It began to look as though, after all, there was not going to be any better start for Maja. In solitary mo-ments between her heavy tasks she sometimes grasped that she was already well on in years, cast up on this kind of farm . . . with Benjamin's flushed old-man's face and drink-sodden mind, long since settled in its mold, un-shakable whatever might happen, for highest authority. And somewhere in between were the cupper-woman and daughters with their own private knowledge, and for spectators the surrounding gray village. So apparently it would go on. . . . Such moments of musing made the tip of her nose droop ever lower; two of her front teeth had already fallen out. Suppose Benjamin were to die, what would become of her, with no heir and so far no hope of one?

Then came the promise of an heir. During that period of waiting Maja's watering eyes often gazed out dreamily from between her pallid cheekbones. Now an heir was on the way; but to that circumstance attached so much compulsory planning — she had to look ahead. The child would have to be nursed and brought up, care taken that its inheritance increased and was not wasted. Each time such thoughts crowded unbidden into Maja's mind, she felt worried. Anything resembling organized planning oppressed and wearied her; she saw in her mind's eye successful and necessary good results, but felt at the same time that these called for calculated efforts and a small steady stream of energy. Maja had already experienced a thousand thousand little hardships in her time; nothing had ever really gone off in her case as it should have done. And now there were Eva and Marke and Benjamin's oldness and all the rest. Why hadn't even her marriage been like that of other girls? Not to have to make any effort, that was what one had to arrive at.

Nature, meanwhile, took no notice of such demands, but went on with its own work. The absolute, exacting continuity of nature on the one hand and human hopes on the other, the core of all life's tragedy, were as much in evidence also in these circumstances as a flower grows true to its species in the loneliest nook of the most godforsaken wilds. But when her hour was upon her, the uncomfortable pressure of Maja's many worries relaxed for a time. She had a sense of arriving at an ideal state. All the Evas and Markes, the Benjamins and cupperwomen — what did they matter?

A tallow candle burned in the room off the bakery at Ollila, and in its yellowish light three men were sitting. Pa Ollila is a man in his sixties, with clean-shaven cheeks and a dense white fringe of beard stretching from ear to ear under his chin. He speaks his own Kokemäki dialect and holds his neck and the trunk of his body always stiffly upright. There is dignity even in the way he drains his glass, and when Benjamin starts to get skittish and tease him, Pa crushes him with calm remorselessness, and Benjamin is afraid to pick a quarrel. For at Pa's side, equally stiff and immobile, is his son Frans, a sturdy bob-haired man in his twenties. Frans, too, lets slip a sentence now and then, gravely, never with a smile. When he speaks, he speaks for himself, yet somehow his remarks always confirm what Pa has last uttered. They drink without becoming intoxicated. Here on their own ground they seem between them to be making Benjamin dance to their tune, Benjamin who is such a tyrant at home.

Kokemäki men have begun to settle in the parish, one here, another there. They are broad-chested, callously disregardful of the proprieties of life in the locality. Dressed in their shawls and sheepskin coats, they call loudly to one another in their own harsh dialect even outside the church.

The candle is nearly at its last flicker, and so is Benjamin Nikila.

" Seems like you can only last out a tallow dip," says Pa Ollila. At the point where Benjamin is beginning to be hazy, Pa is only beginning to warm up. " And it's no use you bearing spite against me because I wouldn't give you that money. How did I know what kind of place you had? . . . and I'll say it again, going and getting married the way you did. . . ."

In his drink-fuddled mind Benjamin sensed the gulf between him and these men, the aggravating superior strength of their personality. It was as though he and his farm with him were already passing into their hands without their even willing that it should be so. Signs of an instinctive irritation began to show in Benjamin. He got up as though intending to do something about it. But at that Pa rose to his feet.

" You get off home with you, neighbor," he said, " and see to your wife. I'm thinking she'll be giving you a little one this very minute."

Pa and Frans led Benjamin out. He found himself in the pitch-dark yard and began making his way, step by step, towards the other end of the village. His eyes stared into the darkness, and as the drink had wiped out all consciousness of his everyday routine, he saw only the stark fundamental features of his life and circumstances in all their unsavoriness. This earth and yonder sky

and those Kokemäki men, no amount of evil temper
could prevail against them. Against all else bad temper
has helped. Dreadfully sickening to feel that things exist
that cannot be overcome by a fighting temper and cannot be ignored. Old Benjamin was near to being crushed
by an obstinate suspicion that there might be things to
compel his respect.

He growled in his throat and sat down by the roadside.

A tiny wooden torch burns in its holder on the living-
room wall at Nikila; its light falls on the two red-haired
daughters, Eva, the older, and Marke, the younger. Both
are the offspring of Benjamin's second marriage, the sole
surviving offspring, and take after their mother in appearance. They have a stolid air and are sparing of
speech even when alone together, yet they always seek
each other's company. This evening the bond of sympathy between them is particularly strong, for all the
evening they have had the living-room in which their
infancy was spent to themselves. With the mistress away
and the master away the servants are not likely to stay
at home, for this is the season of the year for hirings
and sprees. Only the crickets cry continuously in the
cracks of the big brick fireplace and from the split-wood
fire the bark gives a ghostly rustle as it curls into ashes.
Right under the torch-clip Marke sits, mumbling the
words of her long narrow Catechism; farther away Eva

treads her spinning-wheel. Each time Eva stops to move the thread to the next groove, Marke stops reading and would like to say something, but as her sister sets the spinning-wheel whirring again at once, she wets her finger and goes on reading. Marke is still a little childish, unconfirmed, whereas Eva is nearly grown up.

The sole materials of which their mood is composed are the happenings in their little lives and surroundings. When summer wanes, torches are lit in the evenings and winter is nigh. They see this repeated year after year and meanwhile find themselves growing up. Mother died the autumn before last, about this time; Maja now makes herself at home in the house, goes freely to the storerooms and attics, and is going to have a baby; Father is always drunk. The nicest time was the year after Mother's death; Father was nearly always away and when he came home he did not beat them as he used to beat Mother. Eva had the keys and clung to them so well that the cupper-woman got very little at that time, even though she was always prowling around the farm. The cupper-woman talks familiarly to Father and has never been afraid of him even when he is angry.

Marke let the book sink to her lap and tried to talk to her sister.

" Where's Father again? "

" At Ollila, I suppose."

" Why is Lovisa always here? Why is she always laughing like that at Father? "

" The cupper-woman's been his sweetheart once."

" Yes, but why is she still here when Maja's here as well? And what right has Maja to act as she does here? "

" She's the mistress."

" Mother was the mistress."

" Yes, and now it's Maja and she's just going to get a baby, so now you know."

" How'll she get that? And why is she getting it in the bath-house? " Marke persisted.

" Ask Maja," was all the reply she got from her elder sister.

" When are you going to get a baby? "

" Pooh, on the big tomorrow when the cherries ripen," Eva answered with a tired smile, and rising, she put aside the spinning-wheel, yawned, and fingered her hair.

The Nikila girls, small-eyed and red-haired, left all by themselves in the farmhouse, began boredly to prepare for bed. Maja and the cupper-woman, Lovisa, were still in the bath-house, Benjamin, the master, still somewhere in the village. One can well believe that on that pitch-dark night, when the only sound outside was an occasional bellow from a drunken farm-hand in the village, these three groups of human beings unconsciously withdrew deeper away from each other into their several shells. Eva put out the torch, closed the smoke-shutter, and lay down nearest the wall on the creaky bed behind the fireplace, where Marke was waiting to snuggle down tightly beside her. Eva let it happen, though she didn't much like it.

2 0

From the porch came the sound of hasty footsteps. The cupper-woman went into the master's room, then into the bakery, opened the door to the living-room, and was off again. A male child had already arrived in the world and had been bathed and swaddled. While the cupper-woman was fetching a basket, the mother made the sign of the cross over its chest with her hand, muttering a mixture of prayer and incantation. Then with a sigh she lay down again, in her mind and limbs an unaffected sense of happiness and languor. In those moments fear and exertion were absent; for a space she could be alone with her child in the silence of the bath-house.

A mysterious being one hour old breathed audibly in its basket in the Nikila bath-house on the eve of Michaelmas Saturday in a remote dark corner of the earth sixty years before the Red Rebellion. Not a very propitious hour to be born in, if not especially unpropitious; the circumstances were common enough.

In the living-room Eva wakened to the sound of her father stumbling towards his bed. She woke up a second time to hear him grumbling about something until a voice from the bed near the door said: " Stop that nagging now, old fellow, or if I get up to you you'll sure do so."

The voice was that of the farm-hand Abel, who had also come home late.

The old man did shut up for a while, but then got up again and, muttering to himself, went out on the porch, where he could be heard calling for Lovisa. The farm-boy giggled in his bed. All this Eva heard distinctly, finding nothing unusual in it. Marke heard nothing, but slept soundly on, snuggling ever closer to Eva, apparently, in her sleep, mistaking Eva for her mother.

Maja had had her own reasons for hoping for the birth of a child, and after its birth she had experienced those solemn moods which Nature herself brings as a gift. But no sooner are those moods over than the almighty everyday emerges again, and then the birth of a child is usually seen as something respectable folk accept without murmuring and endure with patience; as one of those burdens which life invariably brings with it in one form or another and which lend to human life its gray and slightly wearisome flavor. Should the child die in its infancy its death is more an occasion for rejoicing than its birth had been. The mother sheds tears, but openly admits them to be tears of joy.

When she was not with the child, Maja always remembered that its survival was a matter of importance to her. The thought would then sometimes flash into her mind that Benjamin cared nothing for the child; at such moments new feelings would awake in Maja's breast towards Benjamin. These feelings even began to shine through the exchanges of words between husband and wife. Maja tried instinctively on these occasions to retain the coyly railing tone struck during their courtship, but alone with Benjamin she might recklessly, in bursts of coarse humor, address him familiarly as "thou." This mode of address seemed somehow to appeal to Benjamin; Maja had a feeling that her value and influence were on the increase.

So long as little Jussi was helpless and incapable of adventuring around alone, one day was pretty much like another for him. An old battered cradle stands in the far corner of the living-room. The two-year-old boy lies there in the dusk of evening with his feet in the lap of his stepsister Marke, who has seated herself across the foot end of the cradle. The knots standing out high in the worn floor make the cradle bump as Marke, listlessly crooning, rocks it. The boy will not fall asleep. Every now and then he tries to sit up and cries for his mother, and each time Marke thrusts him down. The child is tormented by the growing darkness and the fleas and bedbugs.

After the boy has risen wailing into a sitting position for the twentieth time, Marke at last struggles to her feet and lifts him out of the cradle, gathering his bowed legs into her arms, and takes him to the window, where a faint daylight still hovers. Seeing people moving in the dusk beside the well and cow-house door, the child grows calmer. Then he falls to wailing again in a steady low tone. A door bangs outside, indoors a cricket creaks, the faithful household spirit of those days, the age of the wooden torch. Marke is by now bored with her own boredom. She gazes with a complete absence of feeling at the tear-stained twisted face in her arms; " Maja's son; Father is its father, too. . . ."

The men come into the living-room, Abel and Gustav, the farm-boy. Mastomäki, the day-laborer, can be seen passing through the gate homeward. Maja's footsteps sound on the porch and die away in the direction of the bakery. The evening has begun.

After Abel has doffed his blouse and spread out his gauntlets and wet rag foot-wrappings by the fireplace to dry, he reaches down a bundle of torches from the rafters, finds a match, strikes it on the plastered fireplace, and lights the torches. The child ceases its low wailing and blinks his eyelids. He is exhausted, but gives a scream the moment Marke tries to set him down in the cradle.

Abel has brought out the makings of a sleigh. Gustav dozes on the bench, idle until expressly told to do something. Now Maja, the mistress, comes into the living-room and in her stride snatches up Jussi to her breast to suckle. Going on three years old, Jussi has not yet been weaned. Maja has simply put off weaning him.

Maja knows her duties as mistress. She orders Gustav and Marke to practise their reading. Gustav goes to fetch his Cathechism, but Marke hesitates. " You wait till your father comes," threatens Maja.

Gustav has just got well into his drone: " Answer, the old Adam, who still dwelleth within us every day — er-er — repentance and improvement — er-er — and all evil lusts — er — shall be drowned and — and each day rise again — er — " when Abel, who wants a good light for the joint he is fitting together, growls at him: " Boy, come and hold a light."

The hiss of a plane, the humming of a spinning-wheel, gabbled lines from the Catechism. Benjamin himself has come into the living-room with a bundle of torch-wood under his arm and begun to whittle torches. He has been sober all day, and on such days the others cannot help noting a certain dignity in him.

A couple of hours later these people of diverse ages are all asleep. Around them sighs the endless, gloomy night of the backwoods, like a single living entity watching over ignorant human beings struggling helplessly in the sea of Time. The fateful '60s have dawned, yet of the dwellers in this house, cast by accident into each other's company, not one has an ear to divine from the cricket's chirping the coming fateful events of those years. Seven separate breathings only steadily assert their right to draw on and give to the joint atmosphere of the room.

The breathing of the youngest is almost inaudible. Little Jussi has at last fallen asleep in his mother's lap and been lowered into the stale-smelling cradle. There the tiny body lies with all its various parts, it, too, struggling unconsciously onward along the sea of Time towards its distant prime and still more distant old age and a death envisaged by none, after which all shall still be as before, the shore of that endless sea still invisible. Flesh, blood, and, hidden inside, bones. But for this particular tiny combination the journey towards death is irksome from the outset. In the invisible cells of the tiny bones a process is already going on, of which no one sees more than the results, the gradual curving of the thigh-bones, the lumpy skull. And as the darkness becomes settled, a bedbug darts with incredible agility from a corner of the cradle and speeds along the coverlet until it finds what it is seeking.

Messages of all these matters keep on arriving in the fragile chambers of the brain. When these messages become agitated a distant voice begins to sound, its waves penetrating into the mysterious activities of all the other brains. But only in one brain does it waken a response.

Maja gets up from her place beside the snoring Benjamin, rubbing her inflamed eyes and scratching her ribs, to rock little Jussi. Jussi, however, is not appeased, but wails louder and tosses on his pallet. At that, Maja bends over the cradle with impatient movements to give him suck. When will the day dawn when she will have to wean him? A feeling of surfeit fills Maja's mind as in that heavy midnight hour she feels the boy draw greedily the meagre juice from her breast. Too tiring in the long run. And she knows that the farm is saddled with debts.

The boy calms down again — for a little while — and a thousand unseen outward and inward influences continue their work, slowly, slowly modeling the tiny being into a human individual. Maja stretches herself out with a sigh on the bed beside Benjamin. Gustav talks in his sleep. Then all is silence save for the breathing of the sleepers. On the ledge of the fireplace a cricket gnaws at the cover of a Catechism that has been left there.

Those days left in Jussi's mind only sensory impressions: a ray of sunlight or moonlight on the floor, scolding voices, the crackle of a burning torch. Then came a day when a Christmas scene, with a canopy of straw suspended from the ceiling, straw on the flood, candles, and hymns, became imprinted on his mind. The first really consecutive memories, however, that were to remain permanently in his mind related to the following events.

He was alone in the big living-room. At the moment he had no definite wish to go anywhere. He had just come from the bakery, where his mother had given him half a cup of coffee. People said of him that he was turned five. He was a boy. Sitting on the floor, he stared at the windows and window-frames. Something seemed to have stopped. Or rather it was as though he had just become aware of something that had always been. Saturday, Sunday, Tuesday. . . .

The clatter of footsteps came from the porch and the next minute Benjamin — Father — was in the room. Old Benjamin and little Jussi face to face; inevitably a momentary unconscious relation formed between the two. A secret inner man unknown to anybody awoke in the depths of Benjamin's being; he seemed to be watching a shy wild animal creeping forth from some ambush. *He has got to do something to that boy.* He looks smiling

2 7

at the child, seizes him, and lifts him on to the ledge of the fireplace.

In his pocket are a few baked turnips. He brings out one and orders the boy to take a bite. The boy obeys, uncertain whether he likes or dislikes what is happening to him. He recognizes the familiar smell of liquor and tobacco and sees Benjamin's hairy face from an unusual angle, level with his own face. A rather dreadful being, Father. . . . The incalculable being is still smiling and doing things. It takes the plug out of its cheek and in slow deliberate fun pokes it into Jussi's mouth. The boy is afraid to resist, to hit out; his mouth twists into a peevish howl. To sodden old Benjamin it brings a tiny sickening pleasure. Maja's boy. . . . A strange brutal desire to do something wicked to Maja as well awakes in him. He cannot quite remember whether he has ever given Maja a proper beating. What with having two wives before her, it is hard to remember which got what. . . .

Maja comes into the living-room just as Benjamin is forcibly thrusting his tobacco-smelling finger into the boy's mouth. She draws nearer, intending to lift the boy down.

" What are you up to now again — drunk? " she asks.

" Nicely, old hag! " Benjamin roars in his hollow old man's voice, in which the rage is patently feigned, and pushes Maja away.

" Swiller, what do you think you're doing to live on next year? Will you let the boy down! "

" Hell's cow, are you going to hold your jaw? " snarls Benjamin turning fiercely to Maja.

Jussi takes advantage of the diversion to jump down from the fireplace ledge, his heels jarring on the floor; and rubbing his lips, he darts out into the yard. Evening is drawing nigh. The cupper-woman's husband, David, is coming through the gate with a birch-bark basket under his arm, his lips pursed in the intent expression of a short-sighted man.

" Father at home? " he croaks.

Jussi does not answer. In David's memory Jussi is hereafter fixed as a wicked brat. David is bringing tobacco-leaves for the master of Nikila, whose own tobacco was nipped by the frost.

A little later Jussi sneaks back into the living-room.

" You've got a good old hag too," Benjamin is remarking, the basket open on his knee. " I know your old hag better than you've ever known her, hey, what? "

" I'll bet you two have your own knowings," squeaks David. " But can you say, master, what we're going to live on next winter? "

" Never mind about that, I'm talking about your old hag. Ever given her a good beating, eh? "

Maja comes into the living-room. Benjamin casts a glance in her direction and catches sight of Jussi.

" Eh, is the lout still here? I'll give him some tobacco." Benjamin's voice, however, sounds good-natured, and Jussi therefore only moves nearer the door. Maja goes out again, slamming the door behind her.

2 9

"What? I'll — " bursts out Benjamin, getting up. Nevertheless he does not follow her, but sinks down slowly on the bench again with a wrathful air.

David makes a new attempt.

" Oh, ay, the poor will need to do some knowing next winter — I suppose you did manage to cut a little rye at Nikila."

"Don't snivel; come and have a drink," barks out Benjamin. David follows him; a drink is something to the good, even if he is put out at his failure to get the old man to join in his lamentations about the bad crops. They go upstairs to the attic.

This chain of events and the impressions left by it remained clear in Jussi's memory; right to the end of his life he would sometimes catch the feel of that afternoon in all its original vividness.

That same evening the cupper-woman's children came to Nikila. Jussi was naughty to them; he spat on the boy, and when the victim ran to tell his father, he was near to getting a thrashing. The evening was one long confusion, but somehow solemn. Later Lovisa came to fetch David. David had by then to be supported home. Lovisa handled him in a very matter-of-fact way; she did not mind people noticing and commenting on her rule of her husband. So long as Lovisa was able to get about, there would be no starving in that home.

The natural order of things was already breaking up at that time. The first serious failure of the crops had hit large areas of Finland hard. But in the '60s the horizons of the sea of Time in which all these different people were being rocked were very, very limited.

During the years that came before the great famine period Maja Nikila's boy Jussi was one of the troop of children that played in the Harjakangas lanes. A big head surmounted his thin neck; the smock left his bow-legs visible. His mouth tended to be always open and his small, hardish eyes often stared unwinkingly around him.

A rocky mound with many folds thrust into the heart of the village. It was the common pasturage for the village pigs, Pig Hill, and the favorite resort of the smallest children. One dilapidated hut with a few apple-trees growing beside it stood on one slope, and big rowans grew here and there. The hut housed a fam-ily with many children, later to become notorious as the Pig Hill lot, the boys all vagrants and rowdies, the girls ill-famed in many ways. There were children also on the Husari and Pelttari farms, the cupper-woman had two, and at Nikila there was Jussi.

In the matter of clothing there was little to distinguish boys from girls. Boys, too, wore loose unbelted smocks until they were about ten. In summer many a child of five still ran about clad only in a shirt, its hair streaming freely. Boys had their hair clipped at the ends, so that from some way off they appeared to be wearing inverted bowls on their heads. When they climbed the rowans and hung head-downward from the branches, the bowls broke up into tangled manes. On clear autumn evenings a group of this kind might be sighted in silhouette from the lonely lane along which the cupper-woman trudged home from Nikila and where stiff-backed Pa Ollila sometimes took a stroll.

The children led a wild, adventurous life; each evening was the close of a long phase of life, the abundance of which later gave rise to the feeling that this period of their lives had been longer than any later period of like measure. The contents of those days the children were at perfect liberty to chose for themselves out of whatever their senses and budding intelligence could find to snatch at between heaven and earth.

One great world was everywhere above and against them — the grown-up world. In that world were included the fields and lands, houses, and even animals. Everywhere these concealed the intentions and purposes of grown-ups, purposes the children were compelled to serve as soon as they were capable of doing so. Grown-ups moved through the lanes, went into the fields carrying implements, came back again, were usually grave, sometimes drunk, and always incredibly contrary in regard to anything a child found important. No grown-up person ever climbed to the summit of Pig Hill. Grown-ups were one of the mysterious problems of nature, always to be feared because now and again they " brought up " children. Bringing up might take any of a number of forms: hair-pulling, wrenching by the arm, beating with a stick, a belt, or a rag slipper. Bringing up was the only occasion on which a grown-up devoted the whole of his attention for the time being to a child, the only occasion on which a child provided grown-ups with a mild thrill of pleasure. For instance, on summer evenings when villagers had assembled in the grassy yards to talk things over and children were at their wildest, the urge to bring up a child might awaken in the bosom of a father or some other person. On such occasions you could not help noticing that the ensuing hiding fascinated the other men; it was obviously one of those matters regarding which a mutual understanding existed between grown-ups. The other men might even vouchsafe a friendly word or two to the victim. After which the men would shove tobacco into their cheeks, spit, and become sternly manlike again.

Only men, and a few women, were real grown-ups. The other women — hags, womenfolk — were, to be sure, a cut above children, but a race apart from men. In their coffee-drinking there was a hint of the forbidden as in some of the children's games. They had their own secret business unknown to their menfolk and were properly subdued when a man flew into a rage. The basic color of their lives was gray, and one element in this grayness was to be occasionally found out by a man. It was part of a real man's life to take notice of his wife's tricks now and then, though it was not correct to be always spying. Real manhood seemed to breathe from that region about the waist where a man's shirt and his belt peeked out. Belted trousers sagging a little in front and behind were the hall-mark of a man. When a male had achieved these he could chew tobacco, drink liquor, go after women, talk bawdy, and use such words as " brat " when speaking of children.

Between smock and belted trousers was the period of combined vest and trousers, the wearer of these being referred to as a lout or in milder fashion as a hobblede-hoy. The most solemn event of the lout period was Confirmation class. Actual participation in Communion service was one of the weird features of the grown-up world, something in the same class as having a child. As soon as a boy had been to Holy Communion, a gulf opened between him and the world of childhood. He quickly slid into the alarming, mysterious, and admired company of grown-ups. Only grinning and in joking fashion would he let fall a few vague hints when those still on the other side of the gulf questioned him about the most secret adult matters.

Yet even these " most secret " matters were not wholly unknown on Pig Hill. The differences between an " old hag " and an " old man " were duly noted, imagination came to the aid of vague suspicions, and many games were played, at first with much giggling, then breath-lessly. Dreadful the thought that these games might come to the knowledge of grown-ups. As some of the children were only just learning to talk, these had first to be conveniently lost. Sometimes one of these three-year-olds would run crying home, with the result that an irate mother might come to find out who had been teas-ing her brat. That brought the game to an untimely

3 4

end, and it might be nearly evening before it could be resumed. . . . But if no interruption occurred, the exciting game might continue and lead farther and farther away from the village, to end in fears of a hiding during a belated return home. These fears would sometimes prove to be well founded, at other times the truant might find at home a genial atmosphere: Father away somewhere and Mother drinking coffee with a neighbor's old woman. That was a pleasant afterglow to the rich experiences of the day.

Jussi passed through the usual phases up to his ninth year. At twenty and even thirty, memories of those Pig Hill days would suddenly crowd into his mind. Not until he had married did he entirely forget them. And when he had children of his own he never, not even by accident, associated them with the games played on Pig Hill.

These games came to an end when Jussi was in his ninth year. That year many other games played beside the thousand lakes came to an end. People read out the figures on the backs of their almanacs, one by one, 1, 8, 6, 6. Some there were, of course, who knew how to read them: one thousand eight hundred and sixty-six.

It rained that summer, rained without ceasing. After St. Jacob's Day hardly a day when rain did not fall on the muddy roads and sodden fields. Old people lamented, the younger were silent, and melancholy children gazed out of dim window-panes, unconsciously

afraid that they would never be able to return to their
playing-fields. To go out was to face a cold wind that
drove the raindrops through one's thin smock; one's toes
began to tingle with the cold and one had to hurry back
to the warmth of the home.

The anxiety in the minds and countenances of adults
was vaguely reflected in the children's minds; they missed
the bright harvest- and sowing-days. The older children
were instinctively quieter as they saw the men bring in,
between showers, the germinating grain and potatoes
dug out of a morass of mud, or work, up to their knees
in clay, at a hopeless autumn sowing. For Jussi Nikila
— and for Maja — there were two happy days that summer, when Benjamin went off to Tampere. The rye
reaped at Nikila was no good for sowing, and so with
what could be squeezed from the cows he went to town
to buy seed. On his return Benjamin had a little seed
grain with him, but not enough. He also brought with
him his first bottled liquor and had contracted his first
debts at the seed-merchant's. Of the small stock of seed
Maja succeeded in stealing part, which she gave to the
ragman in exchange for coffee. This time Benjamin noticed the theft, and a quarrel ensued that lasted two days
and blazed up every now and then into sheer fighting.

Autumn and winter swooped down early on the sown
fields, still only half-protected by snow. At Nikila most
of the land had to be left unsown, and before Christmas
bread was being baked from flour that was more than

half chaff. After All Saints' Day the only males left on the farm were Benjamin and Jussi. The farm-work was left to depend on the two crofters.

In the midst of well-timbered forests these people — the term " Finnish nation " meant nothing to them — struggled on from week to week and month to month, beset by a mounting tide of misfortunes. There came a June when a Harjakangas farmer going out into his yard at three o'clock in the morning would see in the soft reflected light of the clouds snow on the slopes of Pig Hill, gleaming white ice on the lake, and tangled yellow sprouts in the rye-fields. Midsummer and the following weeks were in their sudden bewildering glory like the premature attempts of a sick man to rise from his bed, a turn that boded no good. Then came the first days of September, brightly smiling mornings that seemed to say in answer to the distraught look in men's eyes: " Why this amaze? Can you not see that these are festival days? A new era is dawning."

As though to celebrate the event, nature furnished three such rime-adorned mornings in succession, al-though one would have been ample. People trod the narrow lanes looking strangely shrunken. Among them was Benjamin Nikila, quite sober and comically solemn. He saw men working in Husari's field at a task that at any other time would have provoked ribald remarks from him; they were cutting the sparse rye with scythes and raking up the cut stalks into little bundles of straw.

As it was, Benjamin passed staidly by and with unfeigned gravity said good-morning in a voice not far removed from tears.

After long preparations, like muttered remarks from afar, and taking care the whole time to leave a little room for hope, the dread visitor had come at last and relieved its victims of their torturing burden of hopes. In Harjakangas village Pa Ollila was the only man who harvested a small crop of rye. He did not, however, dwell much on this good fortune, but spoke all the louder as he went about saying: " It's real hard lines to think that it'll be spring before pine-bark will be fit to eat."

Dusk gathers on the last Christmas Eve the Nikila family is to celebrate together. Somehow there is work to be done even in times like these; even on Christmas Eve odd tasks keep the family occupied till nightfall, so that no one has time to let his thoughts dwell at any length on Christmas until darkness forces them to go indoors. Moreover, on this occasion toilers instinctively take special care to keep their thoughts from dwelling overmuch on Christmas. They are for once in no haste to come together in a Yuletide spirit of peace. And yet in the depths of their souls these outwardly rough ignorant beings have inherited through long contact with a melancholy and mysterious nature a secret sensibility; many fancy even now that they hear in the air the beat of the wings of the Christmas angel of their childhood's days. And at that sound the footsteps of a solitary toiler tend to falter and his mind surrenders to the reality of the present: a famine-year Christmas. He tries to linger on out of doors. . . . For others, too, will of course have heard the Christmas angel, and in its passage there seemed to be a dire foreboding that he is loath to let others read in his glance.

Somehow, miraculously, on this of all years, time in its course has led to this evening, Christmas Eve. Frost has not held up the passage of time.

In the twilight old Benjamin sits behind the window in the living-room. He is tired and stares dully into the yard; at the moment he would be unable to pluck up enough spirit for a quarrel. Dread thoughts do not throng his mind, nor has he heard any Christmas angel. He finds it easy to sit idle in the empty room; the prevailing note of his mood is a spiteful boredom.

Christmas — old Benjamin has seen many Christmases, grand ones. The Christmas spirit has coursed richly in his veins, swollen by a satiety of liquor, ale, and pork. At such Christmases a man felt himself master in his own house. His womenfolk and brats were sure scared to death when he set off yelling to the home of his neighbor Husari, that time he was having the law on Husari. They fought to begin with, then swapped horses, and at last slept side by side in Husari's bakery chamber. But it wasn't a long sleep, for early in the morning they drove together to church behind rattling sleigh-bells. . . . There was breadth and depth and height in Christmas in those days. And afterwards came St. Stephen's Night and many others right to Twelfth

Night. Wild Christmases — the old hags were younger then.

In the dusk of a famine-year Christmas old Benjamin dully recalls memories of the good old times. He seems to himself to be alone in the world; for the beings who now fuss about here he feels only a splenetic distaste. They exist merely to witness his degradation, to see him become almost as they are. The cupper-woman still lives, but she is old, and when hags grow old they are as nothing.

Benjamin knows one man who does not lack drink even at this time. Benjamin lets his thoughts dwell on Pa Ollila. An older man than he, yet somehow not of his world, even if he is not of the world of those others either. A man aggravatingly apart, immeasurably above Benjamin and those others in every way. Benjamin knows for certain that Pa Ollila has drunk as much liquor as he has, yet the man is in better health, and richer. Eats mostly bread baked entirely of flour; the frost did not take all his rye, and three full loads came for him from his home parish of Kokemäki. And to crown all, Benjamin owes him money, six hundred rubles. . . . And it's no use starting anything with him on Christmas Eve.

Benjamin got up from the bench and padded into the yard, with no clear idea of where he was going. He saw Jussi shivering with cold on the hillside and was about to bawl at him when a motley company came into view from behind the bath-house, drawing a big sledge.

A familiar scene at this time, one that gives a fillip to Benjamin's thoughts, for the sight of the newcomers makes him realize that compared with them he is after all a landowner, a master.

"A peaceful Christmas," the beggars wish him in a North Finland dialect.

"We want no Northmen's peace here," Benjamin replies. "Pack off with you to Oravainen, the clinic's there. Do you hear? — you're not coming inside when I say no."

Benjamin set off towards Ollila, leaving little Jussi to watch the beggars — or Northmen — retreat. The starving in one's own parish are not called beggars; but as much as fifty years later, during the war, the Juha Toivola that Jussi had meanwhile become still thought of Northmen as aliens of a horrible kind whenever he heard the word mentioned; the atmosphere of this particular Christmas was strongly lodged in his mind.

As soon as Benjamin was at a safe distance, Jussi set off at a trot to the little cabin on Pig Hill. Some instinct drew him away from home even at that late hour; it was as if he expected to find the real Christmas on Pig Hill, one that would certainly not come to Nikila. Ah, if he could spend this evening with the Pig Hill boys! At home Jussi had no companions.

At Pig Hill the arrival of Jussi caused surprise; the mother Gustava, took it for a sign that Benjamin was in bad temper. Tactful inquiries, however, revealed that there had been no quarrel. Benjamin had gone out

4 I

somewhere and Jussi had crept here . . . well, in a way it was easy to understand. Turnip stew lent a flavor of Christmas to the room, but Jussi guessed rightly that he was not to share in it. A shadow fell over his mood; he slipped noiselessly from the room, enigmatical as a Christmas omen. And after this instinctively undertaken excursion there was nothing left to do but go home, away from under the emerging stars. Indoors a torch burned as on other nights. The family was waiting for the master before proceeding to the bath-house. But as the bath-house was cooling, the common steam-bath had to be taken without him.

The Nikila family behaved peculiarly on that evening in other ways as well. Pa Ollila had already let the Christmas peace steal over him; he had bathed and was brushing his beard when Benjamin intruded his company on him. Was this the proper time to talk about debts? And it was too early yet for drinks in honor of Christmas; the right time to begin the row of those was at the supper table with all the farm-folk assembled, after a hymn had been sung. Pa nearly lost his temper.

" You know the sum as well as I do, of course you do. It's six hundred rubles and you've paid no interest at all this two years. That'll go on to the loan. . . .

" You know well enough I don't sell liquor, not for money or on credit. But I'll have the interest added to the loan, as you say. That'll be near enough another two hundred marks. . . .

" For that matter I don't mind giving you a drop of

4 2

liquor for nothing, enough for you to get the feel of Christmas. Got a can or anything with you? . . .

" And don't go bearing a grudge against me if I have to distrain on you for my lawful rights. It'll be two thousand six hundred marks. God's peace."

After the bath there was some anxiety in the Nikila living-room. What would the old man say at their going to the bath-house without waiting for him? Maja was still in the bath-house; she had gone there after the others, having lingered behind to bring in secretly the customary layer of straw for the living-room floor. A poor show the straw made; it was part of a lot plucked that morning for cattle-feed from the thatched roof of a barn and was a couple of years old. Jussi dutifully sat down among the straw, which gave forth a close moldy smell. He felt lonely with only grown-ups around him. A spirit of anxiety had settled on the room.

Old Benjamin's footsteps were recognized while he was still on the porch. His familiar eye gleamed from the doorway with an unusual brightness, his breath came louder than usual, and those in the living-room noticed at once the fair-sized flagon under his arm, which he carried brazenly enough. It was not a vessel belonging to the farm; he must have got it somewhere in the village.

To everybody's surprise Benjamin did not start quarreling at once. All were silent; Jussi had crept away from the straw. Benjamin took the flagon to his own cupboard, slowly drawing the door open and as slowly closing it, after which, without a word, he went out. He staggered as he walked; on special occasions like this, one saw clearly how much Benjamin had aged during these difficult years. Hardly worth while being afraid of any longer. The women gave a short laugh when he was clear of the living-room. Nevertheless, there was enough life left yet in the old screech-owl for him to cast a damper even over this dismal Christmas.

If Benjamin had gone out as mysteriously in similar circumstances three years earlier, there would have been good cause for Abel to go after him to see that the mistress came to no harm in the bath-house. But now Abel had left and those in the living-room knew that Maja could not be in any serious danger. Life in all its forms is at low ebb at Nikila.

One faint attempt at a revival of former days did occur before the meal. Benjamin had started to take a steam-bath and had half undressed himself, but then wearied of the whole business. The mistress left him there and returned to the house, and she had had time to lay the table and bring out from one of her own hiding-places the single tallow dip she had been saving when Benjamin, in shirt-sleeves and barefooted, stumbled into the house and staggered to his cupboard. After three great gulps from the flagon he sank down into a sitting position on his bed, in his brain a dull content that he had the liquor, anyway, even though this was to be his last Christmas in this bitter life and even if he was deeper in debt than he could exactly say. His

4 4

spent forces revived to half-cock. He caught sight of the boy, whom he could never resist tormenting. The lad, however, was too small game for Benjamin just now, with all the family present. His glance fell on the straw.

" Who's been bringing cattle-feed into the house, eh? "

" A lot of difference it makes whether that kind of cattle-feed's here or there," said Maja.

" I'll teach you what difference it makes — hags, cows! " roared Benjamin, and staggered to the table intending first of all to upset the candle. Maja moved the candle out of his reach, whereupon Benjamin sank down on the floor, succeeded in gathering an armful of straw, and tried to carry it out of the house.

" Stop fooling about, you poor body." Maja tried to stop him.

" I'll show those Ollila beggars what we do with our cattle-feed! " Benjamin quavered. But in the ensuing struggle he fell down and hurt his hip. He was unable to get up unaided, and, growling, he submitted at last to being helped up by Maja.

Safely in bed he gasped: " Give me a drink! " And when Maja paid no attention, helpless as he was, he roared in a loud voice: " Give me a drink! "

Maja looked inquiringly at Marke.

" There's some in his cupboard," said Marke carelessly.

Old Benjamin Nikila sleeps and the family sit down to their Christmas Eve fare: coarse chaff cake, watery sour milk, mutton, turnip stew. The solitary dip casts a yellowish light on the lean faces round the table. The frost crackles, bringing a greeting from many other homes where other families are at this moment eating with similar feelings. Men and women with solemn eyes; thin-necked children chewing with difficulty as though each morsel swallowed was accompanied by unseen tears.

The lofty heavens with their stars look down on this phase in the history of a lowly people, watching the efforts it is making to keep alive the flickering flame of life for coming, unforeseen fates, for times happier and times more desperate even than these, two, five decades, centuries ahead. The heavens see immense forests where gold in millions slumbers beside a dying beggar and a flame-eyed lynx. In the clearings the heavens see gray villages, where here a man dreams sated dreams of the farms soon to fall into his hands, there another lies asleep in the knowledge that this is the last Christmas he will ever sleep in his inherited home, and where in packed refuges for vagrants, the clinics, those branches of the nation to which no part has been assigned in coming events slowly disintegrate. So varied are the sights the heavens see huddled together in one common gray harmony; the time of sharpest discord is not yet. But in the substance of earth and heaven forces are already at work, invisible and secret. Christmas Eve in 1867. At this distance the period begins to look extremely interesting, but to those living then it was a drab time. After the meal Maja tried to strike up a hymn, but she began on too low a note and the others were unable to join in. She gave up after a couple of verses.

Jussi's mood was composed of the vague impressions left by his experiences of the day. The childish visit to Pig Hill grew to the dimensions of a Christmas adventure, the smell of turnip stew symbolized a Christmas feast, Father's vagaries served to revive old memories, and after the meal he sat down again on the moldy straw. Sleep came at last to round off the faint illusions awakened by this tiny chain of incidents.

Benjamin had always driven beggars away from the house. But this Christmas the first batch of vagrants to arrive succeeded in gaining a foothold of a kind at Nikila. The family had hardly lain down to sleep when an old woman wormed her way into the living-room with two children whose mother she declared had died on the road. As old Benjamin failed to wake up, they were allowed to spend the night on the musty straw. Their arrival woke Jussi to a semi-conscious state, enough for the picture of these tramps to impress itself on his naked sleep-fogged soul. He had a feeling that the real Christmas had made headway while he had been asleep.

In the morning Benjamin was bad-tempered, but physically so weak that he was incapable of creating any serious disturbance. He quarreled vaguely with the beggars. The old woman stuck up for herself and mothered the two children, wringing almost by main force a drop of milk for them from the scanty stock in the house. She stopped over the next night, ate the Nikila chaff bread with relish, appraising its good points, spoke with much inside knowledge of the general state of the country and of the railroad works about to be begun at Rihimaki, rattled off the names of the various refuges as matters familiar to everybody, gave advice about baking, and in short behaved in every way as a person of superior knowledge. A queer moist beggary smell exuded from her clothes, mingling with the age-old smell of tobacco and earth that was the natural atmosphere of the Nikila living-room. On next day she went off with her rags and the two children in the direction of Tampere.

The last phase had begun for the Nikila household. Thereafter beggars came often and were not driven away. No sooner had they discovered that there was little food in the house than they behaved much as the old woman had done at Christmas; dropped their unavailing prayers and made themselves at home for a day or two. One beggar had a pocketful of beans, and these were cooked and eaten at Nikila. Benjamin tried to be fierce, but in the end ate his own share of them.

The customary discipline of the family relaxed, becoming as it were dissolved in the smell of the beggars, which was already a permanent feature of the house. Jussi saw boys of his own age in abundance; a dim idea of a greater world and of its spirit awoke in his consciousness; that queer smell seemed to be enticing him somewhere. He could roam around the house and yards at his will; nobody took any notice of him. He saw death at close quarters. And before long Jussi began to want to follow the beggars. It was as though he divined that he would soon be leaving, but when?

For old Benjamin the days were full of secret misgivings and self-torment. He had finished the liquor and was ashamed to go to Pa Ollila a second time. Why ashamed? He could not have said. Since Christmas Benjamin had felt an alarming loss of bodily strength, and because of this all kinds of unhappy thoughts had begun to oppress him, especially when he was alone. In solitary moments he seemed to hear an invisible parson holding forth in stern accents. From dealing with the days of Benjamin's youth the preacher went on to incidents during his long rule of the farm and wound up by describing the causes and nature of these years of adversity. The preaching voice became low and gentle as it spoke of matters unintelligible to Benjamin. On one subject it said nothing, but all of a sudden the purpose and meaning of the sermon became clear in a single illuminating flash: it was just because of that one unsaid thing the invisible parson was preaching specifically to him — he was dying, he would not see the times change, for he himself was incapable of change. Would he join the lost in hell? He had never thought of such matters, but descriptions of heaven had always seemed sickly sweet to him. Whenever he had let his thoughts stray in that direction, the mind-picture evoked was that of himself on a deathbed, confessing his sins in a thin effeminate voice. The most sickening situation a tobacco-chewing brandy-smelling man could find himself in.

The only form this side of Benjamin's life had ever taken was that he drove to church with the rest and when in good humor made the same jesting remarks about church matters as about other things. If the parson preached like a man, one could listen to him. But everything that had to do with salvation was in the same class as brats, which you had to put up with in this world, endlessly trying as they were to a man of spirit.

But now an invisible parson preached at Benjamin and wanted him to turn himself into a brat. He is about to die, he is in debt, softened in every way, this very minute a beggar pants on the bench beside the fireplace. The bailiffs will soon be in the house, he can feel that. If real men were to see him now, in this state of mind, they would teasingly take him by the scruff of the neck and shake him, as you shake a brat. Impossible to picture Pa Ollila, that whisker-fringed old fellow, getting into a state like this; all he does is talk his grating Kokemäki dialect.

Suddenly a violent fit of shivering shook Benjamin's body; his brains were sticky with his recent thoughts. He was scared, his lips and hands began to tremble, he was going to be ill. His mind acted automatically; he fetched Pa Ollila's empty flagon from the cupboard and instinctively he thrust the deeds of the farm into his bosom. Then, shivering, he hurried out.

Jussi sees him go and knows that soon something will

happen. He is prepared in advance. He gazes in excitement at the Northerner panting on the bench and casts a glance every now and then out of the window to see whether there are more beggars about. There's one coming now. . . .

But there comes Benjamin, too, the flagon under one arm and five stout loaves under the other. Ollila has never yet sent a hot loaf to Nikila from any of his bakings; he seems to be making up for it now. Again Benjamin's glowing apparition fills the doorway, and the newly arrived beggars look longingly at the bread in the belief that it is intended for distribution. But Benjamin takes his loaves and the flagon to the cupboard. Costly articles, though this time he has got them remarkably easily; he hadn't even needed to ask for them. But now the farm deeds are at Ollila. To Benjamin it is as though a crushing weight has been removed from him; his shivering has given way to a pleasant heat. Now for a lie-down in bed.

"Isn't the master going to give a fellow-pauper anything, seeing he's been helped?" asked the Northerner, who had been in the house since yesterday.

Benjamin, who had not noticed the beggars, is now reminded of them.

"I'll show you fellow-pauper!"

He staggers to his feet and looks around him for a weapon. Fever, drink, and the feeling of liberation brought on by a desperate decision have aroused the old spirit in him. His heart glows: drink in the cupboard

5 1

and an opportunity to clear the house and then lie down in peace. The house and the fields, gone, by God! Gone the foundations of life. He sees Jussi among the beggars and in a flash in one quarter of his consciousness he sees all that part of his life to which Maja belongs; it flickers past him as one long aggravating and revolting mess.

But at the decisive moment the tinkle of many bells comes from outside; the end of a sleigh, a bearskin rug, and a stout dark-complexioned man come into view. The Sheriff has come. The beggars are startled, and Benjamin forgets the great devouring desire of his heart. The augur he has snatched up dangles forgotten in his hand.

The Sheriff grasped the situation without having to ask; in one minute he had bawled out the beggars. An electric silence and a familiar smell were all that was left of them. Benjamin's ears sang. His liberation was proceeding with giant strides: the Sheriff already in the house. Benjamin felt exhausted; quite a festival day this. His rising fever and the dark-skinned Sheriff seemed to belong together, to this irreparable thing that was happening. The backbone of the winter was already broken; the evening sun shone on bluish snowdrifts in which there was a hint of spring. And not a single beggar in sight.

All Benjamin could say to the Sheriff was: " Yes — reckon that's so — two weeks from now at the latest — all right, I'll try. Not feeling quite well. . . ."

In some fashion matters progressed so far that the Sheriff got a drink.

"The old hags might have a drop of coffee. . . ."

"Don't want any, I'm in a hurry."

The sleigh runners squeaked; bells tinkled. Benjamin was left alone in the tempered silence of his inherited home. Now he really was alone. Sudden and agitating experiences had aroused in him a state of mind that was the first and last of its kind in the whole of his life. There was not a grain of spite in him against anything or anybody. His tobacco-stained bristly jaw quivered; he wept, the last of a centuries-long chain of landowners. His recent visit to Ollila was his last outing in the Harjakangas lanes.

That same night he died. His last words were: "I'm not dying as a dog of a farmer dies." He was clearly raving at the time, for he uttered these, the last words of a local gentleman which he used to imitate when in his cups, in a gentle, almost blissful voice.

Little Jussi's dream came true soon after Benjamin's death. The farm was sold at the county offices in Turku for arrears of taxes. Pa Ollila, the biggest creditor, made the highest bid; he put in his youngest son, Anton, as master. Maja had to leave the bare-stripped house, taking her son with her. She did not elect to stay on in her birthplace, where her little life ever since her childhood's days had been so full of disappointments, but after dry-ing her tears decided to try her luck with her brother, who was rumored to be in fairly easy circumstances.

One bright morning Jussi awoke to find his mother carrying odds and ends of property to a sledge outside the door. Maja had somehow managed to obtain a few coffee beans, and of the loaves brought home by Benjamin from Ollila a few crusts were miraculously left. They breakfasted on these and stowed away the rest. Then they set off, and the house lay behind them.

Maja drew the sledge and Jussi pushed at the uprights, dressed in his one-piece vest and trousers and one of Benjamin's coats; Maja wore the other. A springlike sun shone brightly on dazzling snow. When Jussi secretly glanced behind him he saw the beautiful brow of Pig Hill where he had played so many richly satisfying games. He swallowed hard once, and the charm of a vagrant's life slowly turned to melancholy.

The first part of the journey they were alone, and Jussi kept on calling to mind all the people he could remember from the first ten years of his life, people who had latterly scattered and vanished. He remembered Abel and Gustav, Eva and Marke and Father, Benjamin. From this distance and these strange surroundings they all looked queerly alike.

Soon, however, Jussi and Maja had traveling company. When they came to the main road they saw, wherever the land lay open, long unbroken lines of tramps. Most were on foot and hauled piled-up sledges, but one saw occasionally an emaciated horse. A sledge or horse-drawn sleigh invariably formed the nucleus of a little group, and those groups usually kept well together, so that even where the crowd was thickest there was always a gap of a few yards between the groups.

The unwonted sensation of being on a journey awakened a growing excitement that caused even the dragging sense of fatigue to vanish. Towards evening this excitement further increased. The winding, fenced-in road led again over open ground; in the distance a red mile-post was visible and at its foot something black that each passer-by stopped to look at. It was a dead man; beside him stood a bewildered-looking girl in a grown-up woman's clothes.

From the group in front of Maja and Jussi someone said to the girl: " Come on to the village, or the wolves will get you in the night."

But the girl only stood beside the dead man and stared vacantly ahead of her.

At dusk they came to a biggish village, where the little army of vagrants scattered into the different houses. Maja and Jussi went on to a dark porch and tried to open the door. But it was fastened on the inside; there was baking going on in the house, for they could distinctly hear the swish of the dough. After they had rattled the door for some time, a woman opened it slightly ajar and told them where the clinic was. Tramping the dark lanes of the village, they found the building at last, a big drafty cabin, a nest of noisy misery.

They were almost unconscious with fatigue, and Jussi

could not understand a single word of a quarrel that was going on between some women. Maja finally found out what it was all about. One of the women was roasting coffee beside the fire. She had been out to get the beans from a ragman in exchange for a few rags which she had pulled off the body of an old woman who had died just at the moment when the other woman, watching beside the death-bed with similar intentions, had popped out into the yard for a minute. The disappointed claimant now declared that the clothes had been taken off while the old woman was still alive; she had seen her move her jaws even after she had been carried out into the woodshed. Hence the squabble. It looked, however, as though the disappointed woman might soon have a chance to compensate herself for her disappointment; a badly swollen man at the rear of the room was obviously at his last gasp.

Here Maja and Jussi spent their first night. In the morning, still in the grip of the same excitement, they continued their journey, and late at night reached their destination. After drinking a little water they fell asleep. And the next day Maja actually succeeded in arranging matters so that Jussi could stay at Tuorila while she went on to look for suitable work.

It was May already and a beautiful promising spring when Maja was next seen at Tuorila. She arrived in the evening, too weak to give any description of her wanderings. During the night her condition grew worse; she groaned so loudly that she woke up the family. Her son was awakened that he might see her end.

So ended Jussi's childhood.

THE POOR RELATION

As A bright sun rises after a frosty night, so the spring of 1868 broke early and beautiful over the death that had raged and was still raging. Or "rage" is not the word, for none heard its voice. Among the small groups it would leave now and then a wasted man in the fold of a snowdrift beside a fence and lessen the cares of a woman in some backwoods hut, already bereft of her husband, by taking her last fragile child. Even where as many as twelve thousand members of the struggling host were assembled in joint affliction, misery did not, so far as is known, give rise to any disturbances.

Along the sandy slope of the Salpausselkä watershed a multitude of this kind worked on a main artery that was to lead east to that great human nest St. Petersburg. While some dug, others stood behind them waiting for the moment when Death would surrender a spade into new hands. And Death strove to be impartial; it allowed thousands to take their turns at the spades and drop them again, and the keen-eyed valuers experienced an agreeable surprise: that iron artery, in spite of the hard times, cost half a million less than they had estimated.

Death worked silently then, and the thousands lying in their sandy graves must surely have wondered when, exactly fifty years later, they heard in the throbbing of that same iron artery the words: " The cup of suffering is full to the brim " — and remarked: " What, only now? It was pretty full in our days."

The new roseate spring shone also on the former little Jussi Nikila in his new abode. Once he had been accepted into the family, he needed no longer to go hungry. During the whole duration of the famine the bread at Tuorila never contained more than a third part of alien ingredients, and that only on two occasions in the worst winter. The master of Tuorila, it should be explained, had been entrusted with the distribution of public relief contributions in the locality, and when accusing rumors began to be rife, that little face-saving trick of mixing bark with his flour became essential. But there was never any lack of pure bread at Tuorila, and always plenty of dairy produce.

Tuorila was in every respect unlike Nikila, and it was hard to believe that the master, Kalle, was Maja's brother. Kalle was a big, hook-nosed, masterful man who looked on his slovenly sister Maja with aversion. Even Jussi could see that on the two occasions on which he was present at a meeting between brother and sister. Mother was downright servile towards Uncle; she left the farm without hesitation on the second day, only too pleased that the boy was to remain. And when, a couple of months later, she turned up again, she did it with an air of pointing out that she had merely dropped in at a place where she was known for the purpose of dying. And certainly the brother's heart felt lighter at this speedy end to Maja.

Jussi was for long in a state of mild confusion. The farmhouse rooms were spacious and neat, and there were many rooms he was never permitted to see. There was plenty of wholesome food, but coffee, which he had been used to drinking several times a day, was denied him here, though not because there was none. In consequence his wasted body rapidly gained in strength, but his brain was always as though it had gone to sleep; a queer unpleasantly healthy stupor weighed heavily on his whole being. His eyes tended to stare vacantly, and often he was quite innocently unaware that he had just been ordered to do something or other. And when he had to start off on some errand, he was soon fighting to keep back his tears; the place was so strange to him and no one ever explained anything; he was merely given orders. Afraid to ask, he would sometimes stand in the yard until the mistress grew sick of waiting and came briskly out to see " how long he was going to be fetching that milk-pail." Jussi would so willingly have run to fetch it if he had only known where to find it or had understood the

6 3

mistress's order. From those days onward the reputation clung to him that he was a clumsy dolt and rather slow-witted.

Instinct told him what any onlooker could see, that not a single attitude or step of his fitted in harmoniously with his surroundings as he moved about awkwardly in the big bakery at Tuorila, ostensibly helping the mistress. Everything here was so entirely different from what things had been like at Nikila. The master — Mother had spoken of him as Jussi's uncle, but Jussi never got beyond calling him master — there was no understanding him at all. Always somewhere about the farm, always solemn-looking, never drunk, and never even for a wonder yelling at the mistress, let alone striking her. The mistress was not in the least afraid of the master. A strange baffling sense of balance and harmony existed between the two; you could not side with either against the other. When evening came, there was no question of running about anywhere outside of the family circle. With the farm-hands and maids Jussi had very little to do. They slept in their own living-room, he slept in the bakery, and the master and mistress in an inside room. At night, always at the same hour, he had to go to his neat unfriendly bed to continue there the discomfort of the day. His growing muscles felt the need for exercise even when he was most torpid, and a sticky repletion added to his sense of enslavement.

Beggars came to Tuorila, but they were a different lot from those who used to drop in at Nikila. They stood humbly in the doorway or sat in the living-room answering the mistress's questions in a tearful voice. Once the mistress asked a woman her name, and when the woman happened to have the same name as hers, she was given alms. That same day another woman came and volunteered the information that her name was Emma. The mistress laughed and gave her something too, but told her to tell all the other Emmas that that trick wouldn't work any more.

Jussi was queerly shy of the beggars who came here; not for anything would he have dared to approach them. This was because he was now one of the well-fed. Later, old acquaintances began to turn up among the beggars, among them the biggest of the children from the cabin on Pig Hill. The sight of them aroused a feeling of shame in Jussi, and the conversation was forced on both sides. They told Jussi without being asked that the Ollila folk now lorded it at Nikila and that the cupperwoman was ill. But this news only penetrated an outer layer of Jussi's mind, and then but vaguely. And when the children left, Jussi was relieved to see them go.

Summer came; grass covered the ground, and the trees were in leaf. Copper cow-bells clanked in distant pastures, and spring sowings were carried out in fair weather with seed supplied by the Government. Benumbed minds awoke to life and began to feel the need for new thoughts. The man walking behind a harrow pondered closely on the years of terror just past, the better to appreciate the sunny days and sprouting corn of the present. And although still unable fully to grasp the depth of the trials endured, the man already drew an instinctive pleasure from a feeling that the beginning new era would soon lay bare a kind of missing principle that was to give life a new direction and new breadth. And when, halting at the end of a furrow, he saw on the road those unhappy tramps, he was vaguely annoyed that the old era should thus still cast a shadow over the birth of the new.

For the former Jussi Nikila, now known as Jussi Tuorila, this and the following summers were the strangest period of his youth, for he was more alone than at any other time of his life.

The lands where he roamed with the Tuorila cattle were rich in variety of scenery; they were slopes once cultivated by the ancient method of firing. Dense woods of trees with leaves gave the land its character, but hidden away in these were meadows complete with fences and hay-barns. At the bottom of a continuous cleft between mighty banks a tiny brook meandered along its own private course. Up above, along the rims of the banks, birches drooped fathom-long festoons of leaves over hot-smelling ant-heaps as the midday sun shone along the cleft and the cattle lay at their noontide rest. Here, once he had become familiar with the lie of the land, it was pleasant for Jussi to peel twigs for whisks and cut striped walking-sticks. Here there was none of that burden of ignorance that still made life in the house unpleasant. Nor was there anyone at his back to order him about; here he could tend the cattle as he thought best.

His thoughts during the day usually took the direction given them by whatever had chanced to happen in the morning or the preceding evening. Sometimes his mind would be engaged the whole day with the present, with the scene around him and the cattle, weaving visions of the future, mostly with Tuorila, its master, mistress, and other elements for background. Life was good here; he would never leave the place. Father and Mother and all of past and gone Nikila were far away and alien to this place; happily, they had been swept away somewhere. This sunshine was not for them. Viewed from this sunny bank, it seemed perfectly natural that the master and mistress never quarreled. . . . Evening draws nigh. Pleasant to return home with the herd.

But sometimes the evening and morning had again been harder to bear, and the next day stern clouds filled the sky. After dinner a flash of lightning struck quite close, sending young Jussi terror-stricken to the shelter of the nearest hay-barn. God has suddenly arrived in his head, straight from the years at Harjakangas. Tuorila is somewhere far away and altogether of no importance; Father Benjamin has found runaway Jussi and sits in his old seat of power. The lightning flashes like the angry eye of all the dead past, the thunder roars, and crying out aloud, Jussi casts himself in imagination into Maja's lap. Gone the stickiness of this place from Jussi's blood; in the rain the familiar landscape has an ominously strange look. The bleak cruelty of his father, Benjamin, and the weak gentleness of his mother are the dearest treasures of his trembling heart on this distant alien clearing in the hour of danger.

And even after the storm has abated, there is no relief for Jussi today. Two cows are missing. Jussi's breath still comes in gasps after his recent sobbing, and that makes the new outburst of tears flow all the easier; what is going to happen to him if the cows are lost? The bell-cow comes into sight near the edge of the clearing, but it has a wild look and it flees when Jussi approaches it. Wolves! Crying and mouthing burning prayers to God, Jussi, a big lad, sets off running home with his heart in his mouth, stumbling along the wet paths, believing each moment he can hear a wolf worrying the cattle. At twilight Jussi's wailings were overheard by an old fellow from a backwoods cabin, who set out for the Tuorila pastures. He found one of the cows stuck in a bog, and the bell-cow galloping and rumbling around it. Grasping what had happened and seeing that there was no immediate danger, he returned home to fetch a rope. . . .

On those grazing lands Jussi spent several hundred mornings, noons, and evenings, and no two of them were exactly alike. The herd-boy of the '70s was incapable of consciously noting their effect on him, which was to etch an instinctive feeling of rootlessness ever deeper on his mind; the past faded from his memory like a weeks-old dream and for him there was no compelling present. He was neither farm-hand nor son; his place was neither the living-room nor the inside rooms, but still only the bakery.

Then came the eve of the day on which he was to go to Confirmation class. With a scaring excitement mingled a pensively happy fascination, for this was a step towards a new phase of life. At dusk Jussi crept without asking leave into the farm-hands' living-room, which happened to be still empty. He sat there humming a grown-up tune, the coarse words of which strangely caressed his mind. He sat on even after the men had come back from work. The master came in person to take him away, and in his voice was an unfamiliar harshness as he said to Jussi: "What are you doing here?" Jussi seemed to sense in his tone a foretaste of the new phase that was to begin on the morrow.

The bobbed-haired boys sat in the church pews and appeared to be listening to the Rector's explanation of the Holy Trinity. The Rector spoke in a slow and clear voice, in polished theological terms wholly out of relation to the fat-smeared boots and homespun coats of the boys. The precise enunciation of his discourse, its form settled during decades of repetition, was far above the cottage sense of the boys, though the color and measured roll of his voice did create a strong atmosphere of a kind to which the mind has inherited a certain receptivity in the course of generations. Nor were primitive conceptions shaken of a Father, a Son, and a Holy Ghost that looks like a bird. Weren't They all depicted above the many-tendriled opening letters of the Catechism?

Many of the boys have at one time or another known moments of distress when they have cried in burning accents the name of the Lord. That God, too, passes down from generation to generation, not through the mouths of teachers, but through great trials in the dark depths of the people's lives. It throbs in the veins of a father as, word having come, he hurries along a grassy forest track to his cabin in order to be in time to take a dying child into his arms. And when an old grand-dad, after a week of drinking, gives his last groan, it is that God who arrives in mysterious expiation. Little children look gravely on and see that God draw near to big people, and they preserve Him in their memories for coming generations. Often the attributes of God in the imagination are those of Father: old, harsh, respect-awakening.

That God, however, does not appear to the collective soul of Confirmation-class boys. While the classes last, there is so much else to do: lessons to be learned by heart from the Catechism if one means to pass and not be singled out for further improvement; food supplies to be taken care of; one had to watch out lest one disgrace oneself in that company. When the master at one's lodgings was away, one went out in the evenings on mischief bent and roamed the village lanes. If nothing better turned up, there were always other boys to shove, and from lost tempers it was only a step to a real fight. One evening found Jussi sulking by himself apart from the other boys, who were in high spirits, when the Rector happened to pass. And of course the Rector's suspicions fastened on the boy who was without playmates, though he said nothing at the time. His disappearance was a signal for the other boys to set upon Jussi.

"Was your father Benjamin? Was your father Benjamin?" they mocked.

And the next day, when the Rector found out Jussi's ignorance on some point concerning the sacraments he said:

"Thou Johan Benjamin's-son, how dost thou employ thy evenings? Thou walkest the roads and seekest not the Lord's holy wisdom. I say to thee: take heed of this reproof."

The other boys watched the Rector and Jussi with malicious delight.

Confirmation class was for Jussi from beginning to end a period of little and big disappointments, a period wholly lacking in that which had been in his mind when he stood humming those grown-up tunes on the evening before class began. He tried, indeed, to recapture that mood on various evenings when he happened to be alone in the living-room at his lodgings, but with scant success. His young unformed mind was at the stage when an irresistible urge drives one to create a sentimental comprehensive idea of the visible world. But in the foreground of his mind were only Tuorila and this village and, as if it were balanced on the top of these, the tangle of sensations evoked by attendance at Confirmation class.

His sense of being alive expanded, and it was as though he were being compelled to follow suit; a big space seemed to be opening out, which he had to fill. His memories of Nikila with all that he had fancied about Confirmation class would not fit in at all; they seemed rather to shrink when what was needed was that they should expand. He felt uncomfortable and helpless in the big living-room, from the window of which one saw the roofs, gables, and tree-tops of the village in the growing dusk. And common to all his present moods was a sense of something to be done; the idea of shirking or forgetting lost its flavor here. And there was the added fear that he did not at all know how to do that something that had to be done.

The feeling of helplessness reached its climax at the moment when he was about to partake of the Sacrament. He knew that at that moment he ought to be thinking of God, but God was absent; there was only the faint fascination born of the strangeness of the wafer and wine. The Rector, the Pastor, and all the other boys wore an air as though there was no call for God to be present then. The dominating atmosphere seemed to be that this was the ceremonial admittance of the year's class to Holy Communion.

An atmosphere of sated rest hangs over the prosperous village this late summer Sunday afternoon. Tomorrow reaping is to begin at Tuorila.

The servants are all away from home, all except Jussi,

who has none of the liberties of a servant. And yet he is a man, one of the Confirmed — how much that idea seemed to hold while the reality of it was still before him, and how little its realization has brought! He is not actually forbidden to do anything, orders and reproofs are about all he ever hears, but he is fettered by the ruling spirit of the farm. It weighs heavier on him now than in those early days after his arrival; especially since his Confirmation has he become aware of it. Only two weeks ago the master struck him in the hay-field. When, half-crying, he cursed to the other men and threatened that he would leave the farm when the year was up, a crofter remarked:

" Well, well, so Jussi thinks he'll not be hiring out for next year."

" No, Devil take me, I won't," sobbed Jussi.

" It strikes me you haven't been hired out yet for this year," went on the crofter, and Jussi sensed that they were making fun of his threats, that there was something unusual in his position which he had not yet fully grasped.

This Sunday, during the still afternoon, he had happened to find himself alone with the milkmaid in the living-room. The girl, an inveterate chatterbox, talked in quite a friendly tone to Jussi while she combed her hair, although when others were present she would not condescend to waste more than supercilious coarse banter on the silly hobbledehoy. Now, moved by the kindness in this passing intimacy, Jussi plucked up courage to ask her questions of a more and more private nature; for one thing he asked what the men had meant that time in the hay-field. Couldn't he give notice and leave, as Manda herself was doing?

" You know well enough you're not going anywhere," Manda said, holding the comb up against the light to see whether anything had caught in it. " The master took you when times were bad, and you've no rights at all until you come of age."

" When will I be of age, then? "

" Ho, when other people are. When you're twenty-one."

Then Confirmation class meant nothing; one had still to come of age. Jussi's glance darkened. He said to Manda:

" Don't you go either, Manda."

" Oh yes. Here's a girl who's not going to see Kalle Tuorila's Christmas spread," answered Manda, once more her own self, and with head erect she went out of the room into the Sunday freedom of the village.

Jussi was left alone in the living-room, feeling much as he had done during his first weeks on the farm. The pleasure of having passed Confirmation class had gone for ever; an oppressive sense of being still only a child filled his mind; he wanted to be back at Nikila. Twenty-one . . . and only sixteen. How quickly all his good times were over!

Jussi gave a start when the master opened the door.

" Where's Manda gone? "

" I don't know."

" Very well, then you can go and tell the crofters I shall want them here for the harvest." The master reeled off a list of all the cottages in the distant crofters' corner Jussi was to visit. " And mind you behave," he added.

The spirit of Tuorila did not extend far beyond the house. There was no trace of it on the sandy road where Jussi was tramping as the calm summer evening drew nigh. His feet moved lightly, his lips sought to whistle a melody, his mind nurtured an illusion of farm-hand freedom. He would have liked to sing out loud, but the sharp-eyed light dwelling in the pine-tops kept him quiet. Wait until the mist begins to rise from the swamps and the night-bird croaks. . . .

Jussi had never had an outing as happy as this during the whole of his time at Tuorila. The flow of eventide impressions from the neat pine forest further softened his liberated mood. At any rate he was a farm-hand as good as any, a Communicant. What did it matter if he was unable to move elsewhere, wasn't Tuorila one of the best farms in the neighborhood? " I sleep in the living-room now," he mused; " if I could only get a cupboard of my own. . . . The master is my uncle, Mother was his sister; I am staying with relations, I'm more than a farm-hand, I don't have to look for a hiring. . . . A farm-hand's got to go if he isn't wanted. A good thing I can sleep in the living-room, and I'll have that cupboard yet; this is how I'll get it. . . ."

From a rocky mound he caught a sudden glimpse of the widespread crofters' community: fields, fences, dwellings. To the right, against the farthest rim of forest, a red sun, aloof and alone, shed a waning light over the locality, the air of which, from the hill-top, was full of happiness and freedom. " Impossible that anyone down there ever said an unkind word to anyone else; each is free on Sunday evenings to go where he likes, even the children. There are crofts here that employ a farm-hand; if I could get myself hired here! " Jussi decided to linger in the place to the last possible minute.

Rye was being cut, it seemed, at a croft called Rouko; harvesters were working along three plots. Every now and then a back would straighten and a sheaf come flying over a raised head. An old man called for ale; some of the harvesters were clearly drunk. " What if they start fighting? What if someone beats me? " Jussi thought.

Jussi found most of those he was to give orders to at the Rouko harvest-bee. He went up to each of them a little timidly and gave his message in the tone of one repeating a lesson learned by heart. The eyes of one of the men glared ominously, moisture trickled on to his beard, and his mouth took on a queer twist as he listened to Jussi.

" Has Kalle's rye started to shake off the ear? " he asked in an aggrieved voice.

" It's not dropping yet, but —" Jussi answered shyly, a little alarmed. Nobody, however, bothered to tease him. He went back to the road to continue his journey to those crofts whose tenants he had not met here.

The night is cool. A harvest-dance is on at Rouko, and Jussi Tuorila is still there. At the farthermost croft to which he carried his message he was joined by one of his comrades at Confirmation class, who persuaded him to come back to Rouko. The cottage living-room is full of dim bustle and ale-thickened voices; a delightful place for a lad unexpectedly at his first dance to enjoy from a safe corner. The living-room is sizable; room enough for dancing and for the violin to sound bravely. How much there is in the world higher and bigger than the spirit that dwells on Tuorila farm! What would the master and mistress of Tuorila be at this dance? Totally out of the picture, figures to laugh at. Whereas Jussi, he is wonderfully at home. He has been out into the yard several times, and no one has teased him; he has even been asked who are to take part in the harvesting at Tuorila. He has been given ale, like the rest, and has tried a polka on the floor with another boy, and means to have another try. Nobody pays any attention to the fact that he is all this time carrying out his errand. A delicious night, far more delicious than any previous night.

Yet time and again Jussi has to slip outside and there assure himself that he has faithfully carried out all the master's orders to the letter. Standing there, he sees in the twilit night the hill from which he first looked down on this spot in the now distant afternoon. At Tuorila everybody will be asleep; the master will not know what time he came home and cannot scold him. Manda is here, and he need not leave until Manda leaves. He goes back to the house and takes his turn at the ale-tankard. He is a man, a Communion-goer, damn it all; Tuorila's old man can say what he likes.

Still, he wouldn't mind leaving now, only he can't go all that way through the forest alone, and Manda is still keen on dancing. It looks as though Manda had no intention of coming with him. Whenever he steals near her and tries to speak, she pretends not to hear. She sits on men's knees. Is she going to be somebody's old woman?

At midnight Jussi is on his way home along the sandy pine-bordered track that leads back to Tuorila. But this time he is not alone. Manda is with him and another girl from the village and five men. Jussi is the sixth male, but he is under no delusion that he is a man yet. When the men start teasing the girls and he tries to be bold with Manda, she says to him pettishly: " None of your impudence. You're too big to suck and not big enough to lie beside a woman for anything else." Jussi feels that his presence is an embarrassment to the rest of the company; the others tolerate him only because he understands nothing.

Yet he is not so ignorant as all that. This night of the

dance he has come much nearer to many matters that he has often thought of while waiting for sleep to come. He realizes that the games played on Pig Hill were sickening children's fooling.

They enter the village. Jussi's heart beats painfully; he senses that the others are in some way against the Tuorila family. The spirit of the farm begins to make itself felt again; it rises and becomes menacing, while the image of the recent dance shrinks to insignificance, retreating as though afraid of something. And now Jussi realizes that he has tasted ale, now that its influence is waning. If he had the choice he would be fast asleep in his bed after a speedy return from his errand. The coolness of the night, want of sleep, and even hunger begin to tell on him, and the company he is in is almost downright inimical to the whippersnapper he is. No more dances.

But when the company makes its way to the row of storehouses at Tuorila, Jussi is unable to break away, not though Manda tells him in fairly coarse language to be off. The men tumble the girls about, and one tries to remove the ladder leading up to the row of little attics, in one of which Manda sleeps, with the result that it comes down with a crash that echoes over the whole farm. The men scatter in all directions as the dark form of the master appears in the bakery doorway. He dashes out towards the storehouses, a stout stick in his hand. Only Manda has stood her ground; the men have escaped and

Jussi has dived under the granary. The master calls him angrily by name, but does not deign to search for him. Jussi hears the encounter between master and maid.

" My week-days and work are yours, my Sundays and nights are my own," Manda says grandly.

Jussi waited until he had heard the master go back to the house and Manda climb to her attic before creeping towards the house. Suddenly, however, there was the master before him, the stick still in his hand.

" So that's the way," and with these words the master seized Jussi by the scruff of the neck and struck him twice on the buttocks with all his strength. Jussi's erstwhile companions heard his howls with an unpleasant gripping at their stomachs. It was not pity for Jussi; they were abashed by their own lack of courage in not defying the master. They meant, however, to make a new attempt later on to reach Manda's attic.

Jussi clenched his teeth to keep back his sobs as he lay in bed. A pang of shame shot through him every time the weals left by the stick made themselves felt. Confusedly mingled in his mind were his childhood at Nikila, his life at Tuorila, the thoughts awakened by Confirmation class, and memories of the dance. " What is going to happen to me in the end? " he wondered.

What actually happened to him next was that he was put to tying sheaves in the rye-field and had to listen all day to mischievous hints about his adventures of the night before. When the rye had been harvested he was

put to threshing, then to plowing, after that to collecting
fence posts, and so life went on. Soon the days were becoming wintry and there were twigs to be cut and the
manure to be mixed. " What is going to happen to me
in the end? " This fundamental problem of Jussi's life
kept on recurring to him each time he bruised some
corner of his being on his surroundings and sulked in
silence.

The world meanwhile went on, with Tuorila in advance of the other farms. A great gap loomed between
household life at Tuorila and at, for instance, Nikila.
At Tuorila there were two rows of dwellings; in one
were the farm-hands' living-room, another living-room,
a kitchen, and two rooms where the old mistress and her
unmarried daughter lived; in the other row were the
bakery, the master's and mistress's room, and behind
this rooms of growing magnificence where parsons and
other such visitors were taken. Both the farm-hands'
room and the bakery were now lit in the evening with
oil lamps, the steady light of which drove the ancient
little familiar spirits even from the farthest corners.
Once a peddler spent the night on the farm, a queerly
cunning old fellow incapable even by mistake of giving
a straightforward answer. His pack contained fancy pins
and printed ballad sheets. Not a subject cropped up
but he had the last decisive word; only when the talk
turned to his own person did he become aggravatingly
uncommunicative. The farm-hand David, who knew as
well as anybody that trickery is what keeps the world

going, tried to pull the old chap down a peg or two by referring offhand to the St. Petersburg railway, with the labor camps of which he was only too well acquainted, and quoting one of the foremen.

" Ay, Vänttinen's the man you mean," said the old fellow like a shot.

And with that there arose a secret competition between David and the old peddler, each trying to show that he knew more of all the doings behind the scenes than the other; in particular, more about Vänttinen, who used to have dead men on his pay roll.

Through the talk shone glimpses of a wider world. Whenever a silence happened to fall, it was as though one heard far off the murmur of an approaching new age. The farm-hands filed out to the bakery for supper, the seeds of a new confidence in their minds; David seemed in some fashion to be a bigger man than the master. But when they came into the bakery they caught a glimpse of the master in the adjoining room putting down a newspaper. The name SUOMETAR stood at the top of the sheet.

A deeper man after all than the peddler, and a bigger man than David. Why the master will not sell his forest, although buyers keep on turning up at the farm, no one can understand. Even Tavela has sold his now and got over a thousand marks for it — over a thousand. . . . And yet Tuorila is always abusing the crofters for wasting his forest. Does that mean that one can get more for a forest than over a thousand?

The master has begun to allow Jussi a little more rope; the lad leads almost the same life as the other farm-hands. His body grows and becomes tougher, but his mind remains unchanged. He can now carry out the everyday tasks entrusted to him without seriously bungling them. Yet he always has an instinctive feeling that the master does not like him. When his first attempt at a milkpail has to be thrown into the fire, the master does not fly into a rage, but merely smiles sourly. And if anyone suggests Jussi for a task that calls for care, the master grins faintly. The master hates in Jussi the inferior strain in his own blood. And his present attitude weighs heavier on Jussi's spirits than the former severity. He is conscious every moment that his departure from Tuorila would be welcomed. Only where is he to go?

The unsympathetic attitude of his guardians makes Jussi move with caution; he tries to keep as much as possible in the background. Sundays are the worst days, for he is not sure whether he has the right to leave the farm, and in the house he is too much in sight. After breakfast is over and working boots have been duly tarred, the other men go out into the village, leaving Jussi alone in the Sunday silence of the living-room, disturbed only by the visits at long intervals of a lame pauper. All he can think of to do are infantile tests of skill intended to test the capacities of little children, and in the circumstances he can work up no interest in them; he merely does them because there is nothing else to do. The mistress comes from her own part of the house to

8 3

see whether the living-room has been properly swept and the sheets changed on the beds. On her departure she absently orders Jussi to take a book and read, speaking with her face turned away simply because she feels that she has to say something.

By the time Christmas was near, Jussi knew that he was not to be sent away that year, at any rate. The Christmas holidays seemed interminable. On one of the minor festival days students from the capital gave a play in the church village. The master and mistress of Tuorila drove there behind tinkling sleigh-bells. In their absence Jussi broke into song in the living-room and tried a few polka-steps. Later in the day he set out boldly for a neighboring farm, in his pocket a few prune stones, which he sucked at intervals. The neighbor's farmhouse was small and old-fashioned, rather like old Nikila. The walls and ceiling of the living-room were lined, in accordance with ancient Christmas custom, with gleaming white shingles; a tablecloth had been spread on the table, and on it were a ham, a platter of bread, and a tankard of ale; hung over these was a straw balda-quin. The master was a mild, pleasant-spoken man who addressed Jussi as Juha and treated him as a guest. Out-side, the cheery sound of sleigh-bells rang out now and then on the road; the mulled ale awakened in Jussi a long-dormant sense of confidence.

Jussi was not sent away from Tuorila even after the Christmas holidays were over, not that spring nor when summer came. When it at last happened, autumn was nigh.

Tuorila did not sell his forest without proper precautions as so many other farmers did in those days. He compared the forest sold by Tavela with his own and had another look at Tavela's timber when it lay in great stacks waiting for the ice to break up. He, too, intended to sell but he bided his time. The result was that most forests in the vicinity had already undergone a first cutting when he made his bargain. The price Tuorila was able to obtain by these tactics astonished everybody and fixed the attention of the parish on this shrewd fellow. One might say that that first sale of forest marked the beginning of Kalle, or, as he began to write it, " Karl," Tuorila's rise as a local pillar of society.

Another result of the sale was, in a way, Jussi's expulsion from Tuorila.

The master and mistress of Tuorila were feeling at this time the urge of a personal ambition. Since the famine years they had rapidly grown richer, and after the sale of their forest their means had doubled. The acquisition of wealth is, when all's said and done, worldly happiness in its most tangible form, and happiness invariably betokens a test. The question is posed: are you man enough to stand happiness? The Tuorila couple found themselves drawn more and more into the best social circles in the parish, in which the influence of the growing Finnish national movement was making itself felt. The Tuorila couple were not slow to grasp the full implications of the movement, and the perspectives it opened were instinctively interpreted by husband and wife as a rise in their social value. In the light of the national movement even forest prices acquired a new significance; wealth became, as it were, ennobled when it could be looked on as an accretion of power to the movement. For the master and mistress of Tuorila the period was a time of silent suppressed bliss.

Such feelings, however, demand an outlet; one had only to take care that the outlet chosen was sufficiently dignified. The matter was carefully thrashed out in the course of many confidential moments between the couple, until on the threshold of autumn they decided that they would hold a celebration at Tuorila, to which they would invite, besides their equals, such of the gentry as might be expected to respond to invitations of this kind. There were, it should be explained, various Swedish-speaking families in the parish with tongue-twisting names and offended countenances who had never been seen at any farmers' celebrations. Even among the accessible were a few with Swedish sympathies, but good-natured and company-loving enough to accept with pleasure invitations to gatherings where they could drink toddy and argue the language question with supporters of Snellman, the leader of the Finnish national movement, and the Finnish language.

8 6

On the day the guests were to arrive, threshing was going on at Tuorila, but after dinner Jussi was told to stay at home and make himself presentable, in order to take charge of the visitors' horses and look after them.

The weather was uncertain, half-cloudy. Jussi hung about the yard waiting, oppressed again by that feeling of discomfort and of being an outsider which the Tuorila household had the power of awakening in him. He was not quite sure yet what his duties were to be; all he knew was that his discomfort had its source in this plan of the master's.

The thought recurred to him that the master was his uncle, his mother's brother. It had recurred to him with growing frequency all the time the upward career of the Tuorila family had set its stamp on the atmosphere of the farm. It was as though the master was somehow improperly climbing out of reach, taking care to avoid looking Jussi in the eye, although Jussi was his nephew. On one occasion that summer Jussi had already gone so far as to make use of a suitable cue to refer in a casual man's tone to the master's grand bargain with the forest-buyers. The master had turned on him an open, almost a kind stare that affected Jussi worse than a box on the ear would have done. And now the master had contrived this feast and made Jussi change his clothes in the middle of the day. The master himself prowled around, shaven and wearing a coat with tails, a look on his face as he walked past Jussi that seemed to say that it had been arranged in advance that Jussi was not to open his mouth on the subject.

The first guest to arrive was the churchwarden, top-hatted and white-collared, and his wife. From the back seat of their cart Konanteri, a homeless university graduate who moved from family to family in the parish, jumped down; he had happened to be soberer than usual and, wanting to be where drinks were to be had, had forced himself on the churchwarden. They were joined almost at once by the Pastor of an outlying chapel, a black-capped surly-looking old fellow in worn clothes; he had married his servant-maid and was therefore not in the habit of taking his wife with him. The next to come was the wolf-bailiff, a farmer who had learned Swedish and was hated and feared by the poor. Soon most of the people whom the parish ancients still remember and whose peculiarities they are fond of describing were present.

Jussi took charge of the horses, put hay and water before them as needed, examined the vehicles, comparing them with one another and feeling the whole time that this job of his was a silly one and probably not at all what he ought to have made of it. Only after dusk had fallen and the noises from the house had gained in loudness did he feel easier in his mind, especially after spectators had begun to prowl round the house. Lads from the crofters' community whose acquaintance he had made turned up, and with them was Gustav Toivola, a youth from a forest cabin some way off who had been to Confirmation class with Jussi. Cautiously giggling, they watched Konanteri being forcibly led out of the main door and listened to his sobbing as he lay beside the potato-cellar. A little later one of the gentlemen came out and scolded Konanteri in Swedish. Konanteri wept and answered in Finnish that none in that company were worthy of blacking Snellman's boots. Who was Snellman? The boys had never heard of any gentleman of that name in the parish.

Jussi had had nothing to eat since dinner; hunger and drowsiness had been assailing him for some time, but in this backyard company he soon forgot his troubles. As belonging to the household, he felt himself the equal, to say the least, of any of the other youths, and as the evening wore on, this sensation began to exercise on him a fascination of quite a new kind. In the excitement of the festive night he experienced for the first time in his life, at the age of seventeen, a feeling of individual independence. For some inexplicable reason, as his companions jostled each other around him, the idea flashed into his mind that he was capable of looking after himself in the world. He had been so and so many years at Tuorila, he had had such and such experiences; now they were feasting inside and he had nothing in common with those making merry inside, but plenty with these outside. A faint malice and a strange fearlessness filled him as he joked with the lads who had come to look on. He was livelier and noisier than ever before.

Meanwhile he went with Gustav Toivola into the

living-room. There, too, their eyes sought for opportunities for fresh mischief, but then with a slight shock they perceived Konanteri fast asleep in Jussi's bed. They crept nearer to study for once at their leisure what a gentleman really looked like at close quarters; for Konanteri was a real gentleman even if he was sometimes off his nut; he had drunk himself out of his schoolmaster's job. He had had more schooling, however, than the Sheriff; nearly as much as the Rector. Look out, he's opening his eyes! The boys crept out of the living-room again and side by side made a dash for the safety of the yard, from where the other youths had meanwhile vanished.

They had become friends. Gustav Toivola's brown eyes gleamed under the brim of his hat, and the coming Jussi Toivola asked him all kinds of questions with the freedom of old acquaintance. A road is soon going to be cut into the Tuorila forests in readiness for the log-haulers next winter; Gustav means to get work on the road. Dazzled by the spirit of liberty that emanates from Gustav, Jussi wanted to hear more, but Gustav, instinctively trying to increase his importance in his companion's eyes, would say no more, but began looking around him for a chance to play a trick on somebody. His glance fell on the wheels of a trap. With a crafty look in his eyes he asked Jussi:

" Do you know where the wrench is? "

" Of course I do."

When the wrench had been found, Gustav proceeded to unscrew the nuts holding the wheels to the axle. He did not remove them, but left them loosely fast by a thread or two, nor did he work on both wheels of any pair, but only on one. Jussi looked on ejaculating: " What the heck . . ." But Gustav took no notice and went on with his work. And when the last vehicle had been dealt with he threw away the wrench and suddenly made off into the darkness.

Jussi was on the whole dissatisfied with this prank of Gustav's. He saw what it would lead to, and he was scared and wondered whether it wouldn't be best to follow Gustav's example and run away. Soon, however, he was searching for the wrench, and, having found it, he began hastily tightening the nuts, pausing every now and then to listen. He managed to give a few turns to most of them, but at least two wheels were still left when he had to make his escape. The first guests to leave were already making for their horses. He reached the living-room unseen. Konanteri was still in his bed and he was forced to seek the maid's bed behind the chimney. Crouched down there, he listened, his heart thudding, for the inevitable outcry, as one waits for an explosion. But time passed, and all he heard was the ticking of the clock and Konanteri's breathing — Konanteri's, who had wept awhile ago on behalf of some unknown Snellman.

At last he heard the master's footsteps. The door opened and a voice asked:

" Is David there? "

No answer from the living-room. David was away on business of his own and Jussi kept quiet. The master came into the room, far enough for him to catch sight of Jussi, at whom he silently shook his fist and gnashed his teeth. Then he was gone, and Jussi was left to crouch on the bed and wait. The idea of running away never occurred to him now.

Half an hour elapsed before the master returned. He came and, seizing Jussi by the hair, jerked him on to the floor. And when Jussi tried in self-defense to cling to his arms, he said:

"So you'd fight, would you?"

The master was in such a rage that he nearly wept. This miserable end to the evening boded ill for his secret dreams, which had circled all through the evening on the approaching Diet elections. At the first bend in the road a wheel had come off the Rector's trap and the Rector had been badly hurt in the spill. The churchwarden's wheel came off as he was climbing to his seat, and that incident was the wolf-bailiff's salvation, for he was prompted to examine his cart in time. The festivities at Tuorila had suddenly lost all their glamour. And it was all Jussi's fault, Jussi's, that wretched lout's, whom the master had kept for years, his vacant face a constant secret stumbling-block in the path of ambitious dreams, a reminder of the master's own former lowliness.

The struggle between the master and Jussi woke up Konanteri.

"Well now, I do believe I'm in that lad's bed," muttered Konanteri with drowsy good nature.

"You lie there as long as you like. That bed's vacant

now," the master said. Thrusting Jussi out of the room, he added: " See, there's your road, the road you came by, back to where you came from."

Daylight had come by the time Jussi was on the last lap of his tramp to Toivola, a cabin in the backwoods. Naked spruce roots, thick as a man's waist, hung snakily over the yielding track, which the sun was streaking with its early morning beams. The hiding Jussi had received had left behind it nothing like the same bitterness as on that former occasion a year ago, after the dance. He kept on repeating to himself, his mind fixed on an image of Tuorila: " I'll show you yet — you just wait." Saying that kept his courage up, though he had no clear idea of what he was going to show Tuorila. Hunger and agitation tempered his spirit and tended to bring tears to the eye of the cursing seventeen-year-old man. The misty backwoods landscape seemed at that early hour to reveal little traits familiar to him from childhood.

He had reached that stage of his youth when anyone who had known him as a child would still recognize him, while those who knew him during the last years of his life might equally easily have recognized him at a first glance. He took, as it were, the first decisive steps towards the fate that awaited him far ahead in the future.

TOWARDS MANHOOD

 JUSSI was not exactly made welcome to Toivola. The hour was early enough for the family to be still in bed, and when the visitor was recognized as Jussi Tuorila, the idea spread that something must be wrong. Jussi had to give repeated assurances that nothing was wrong.

" What's brought you, then? "

" Nothing special," Jussi answered, smiling in an embarrassed manner, and that was all he could find to say. Mina, the mother, had hastily pulled on a skirt and was fast losing her temper. Gustav had been out last night somewhere in the direction of Tuorila. Mina stared suspiciously at the bed where the lad, in an early morning posture, was still asleep.

" What have you louts been up to now? " she asked. The Toivola cabin stood on land belonging to Tuorila; one had to be careful.

The master of the house, an old, weak-looking, wizened fellow, looked on from his bed and had apparently made up his mind to have nothing whatever to do with the matter. Mina went on wondering to herself; Jussi wriggled and smiled, but was unable to give any satisfactory explanation. He was worried by Mina's stubborn surprise; why couldn't she let him feel at home? Everything would settle down all right then. At last Mina said:

"Well, stretch yourself there beside the old man, wherever you come from." And she set about completing her toilet.

Jussi took off his boots and coat and lay down on the space newly vacated by Mina. He lay there beside the silent old man in the wretched cabin which he had entered before this only to bring, as from a higher world, a message from the master of Tuorila. The sleepless night and his many unusual experiences combined to lend to all his thoughts an air of not belonging to him; the compulsory relation in which he suddenly found himself to this dwelling was distasteful to him — almost he regretted what had happened.

Just as sleep began to pervade his consciousness he saw his old home Nikila, lifelike and unchanged. His weary brain evoked the mirage in self-defense, for its own rest and to release for a moment his blindly struggling soul from the associations of the recent past, and earlier, in which it had continuously been fettered all through the long years since the moment when the sledge was being loaded in front of the Nikila farmhouse one morning in the great winter of death. So long ago that had been.

Jussi slept, a deeper sleep than he had known for seven years. And soon he " saw " no more dreams, yet deep, deeper even than the dream-plane of his mind, poignant currents flowed from the present to what once had been. It was as though his deepest ego were moving backwards towards the future.

The personal history of the subject of this tale had reached a major crisis; he had to begin life over again from a new starting-point. Before him were long, vain years leading to coming alien times; Jussi's life had reached a point at which it might as well have ended. . . .

He slept without a break until evening. When consciousness slowly returned to him, he noted first that he was half-dressed, and then that around him was a strange unnatural atmosphere; it was not morning. The mysterious old master of the house was sitting on the fireside bench, and Mina was fussing about and relating some long history. The sons, Gustav and his older brother Isak, were eating, having apparently just returned from somewhere. At once Jussi became aware again of the curious relation in which he stood to the people and life of this house; he was compelled to look up even to people living as modestly as this. He had wakened so silently that no one appeared to be aware that he was awake, and instinctively he made a sleepy movement and pretended to be deep in slumber again.

Mina was speaking in a confidential voice:

". . . He's there, at our place — I says to him — but

I came to see what — I mean to say I'm not keeping any-body's farm-hands — I says — "

" Ay, and what did the boss say to that? " asked Isak with his head in a can of sour milk.

" All he said was that he didn't care where a rascal like that had gone, but I says to him, surely you can't be thinking of driving your own flesh and blood on to the road like that, with only the rags he's got on him to wear — I says — happen he'll have other clothes as well, in case he finds a job of some kind — I says — and I'm surely not expected to give him bed and board for nothing — I says — he'll not be going anywhere from our place today at any rate, so that if there's anything I can take him — I says . . ."

This news interested Jussi as soon as he became aware that Mina had been to Tuorila; that suspense was over, it seemed. Mina had even brought his clothes. But she said nothing about unscrewing wheels. And Gustav merely went on eating.

Isak asked: " Didn't he give you any money? "

Jussi kept his eyes shut, but he felt Mina's glance rest on the bed before she answered in an altered tone:

" I did say to the master that the right thing would be to pay the boy a penny or two. Master tried to put me off by saying Jussi could come and talk about wages himself, but I says to that, you won't catch that boy com-ing here any more — I says — and then the mistress went and fetched this twenty marks. But it's no use giving it . . ."

Mina made a gesture towards the bed and was silent for a moment. Then, in her usual tone, she went on:

" But what do you think to that, going and loosening the nuts on dozens of wheels — fancy thinking of such a thing — a lout like a sleeping man's prayer when it comes to anything else, you wouldn't think he'd have thought of such a thing. Sure you weren't there last night, Gustav? For the day you start such games, I'll . . ."

" I haven't touched anybody's nuts," Gustav answered in a surly tone.

Jussi pretended to be waking up; he stretched himself, gasped, and smacked his lips. Mina looked in the direction of the bed, an expression on her face wholly out of keeping with her latest remark.

" Ah, the champion nut-opener's going to begin his day, I see."

Mina's account of her visit to Tuorila made Jussi feel more of a stranger than ever among these people. In spite of everything, the seven years he had spent at Tuorila had left their mark on him. These were poor people, with a bent for treachery. Even Gustav now seemed very distant, and it looked as though Gustav would have preferred to see Jussi anywhere else than in his home. If only he knew where to go. — But Mina had the twenty marks sent him from Tuorila.

Jussi was given coffee and he then had his supper alone. He had not eaten anything for over a day, yet every morsel he ate seemed to stick in his throat. A couch was made up for him on a bench beneath the side-window. It was hard and narrow; again no question of undressing. Yet in spite of having slept all through the day he was in such a state of lassitude that he fell asleep almost at once. But when in the night he fell on to the floor, he lay awake for long, gazing at the turgid dark autumn sky and listening to the sound of breathing, in which was the same surfeiting alien note as in so much else. In the watches of the night he found no difficulty in seeing clearly, for the first time, exactly what had befallen him.

Toivola was a solitary cabin in the middle of the large tract of forest Tuorila had sold on such favorable terms. Cutting was to begin here already before Christmas. At Toivola the beginning of the forest work was eagerly awaited, partly because of the employment it would bring, partly because life would become livelier when the lumbermen assembled. Mina was secretly annoyed because she was so old — if only she had been so and so many years younger . . . But even now she would see her way to making a bit.

Jussi was permitted to stay on in the house. A new cabin was being built at one side of the yard; the roof, walls, and fireplace were ready, only the windows and floor remained to be done. Isak had begun, when the autumn weather set in, to put the cabin little by little in order, and Jussi was now set to help him. Glib-tongued Mina made it clear to him, however, that such trifling jobs in no way made up for the cost of boarding him, but as there were hopes that he might soon be earning money on his own, she was willing to stake him for the time being. When he started to get wages he could make up for these weeks as well. Jussi listened to her chatter, weary of his whole existence, and lay awake nights, sick at heart.

Then one Sunday after church-time life at Toivola was suddenly transformed. Within a couple of hours nearly fifty men, equipped with provisions, saws, and axes, arrived at the house. In the yard was a great bustle as a dozen or so horses and heavily laden sleighs were being temporarily put up there. Odds and ends in the way of the sleighs were thrown aside; there was a babble of strange dialects. A short, fresh-complexioned foreman came into the house and while still on the threshold began shouting in such a loud voice that even everlastingly silent old man Toivola was startled and mumbled a few incomprehensible words.

"Well, Mammy, is the coffee-pot hot? — for you've got visitors," the foreman bawled.

"I don't remember inviting anyone special today," Mina answered in the tone she would have used if she really had been twenty years younger.

"The best visitors never wait for invitations."

Before evening the Toivola cabin had lost whatever individuality of its own it may have had. The queerly cross attitude towards the men which Mina had seen fit to adopt right from the beginning made no difference. The strangers made no effort to acquaint themselves with the habits of the household. It was curious to hear a newcomer loudly and blithely accost " Pa," that silent dummy to whom no one in ordinary circumstances ever addressed a word. When, later in the evening, Mina began ostentatiously taking stock of her belongings, she was told outright that no one in that crowd had longer fingers than was necessary, and that if any fingers did show a tendency to grow long, they would be cut off, no matter whose they were.

The first night was the hardest; the living-room and bath-house were packed to the limit.

" A tight fit," observed the foreman as he lay down on the straw, " but there's a good cabin in the yard only waiting for the finishing touches to be put to it."

In the morning a surprise awaited the Toivola family. The whole forest gang was put to work on the unfinished cabin. Someone had heard that the glass from the old church windows was for sale, with the result that the foreman — Keinonen his name turned out to be — at once went off to buy a supply. Before evening the new Toivola cabin was being warmed for the first time, and that night most of the men slept there.

The following morning there was a general move to see " what kind of pines Pa Tuorila has been growing for Pa Rosenlev." In the living-room Mina snapped at Jussi in the foreman's hearing:

" Well, aren't you going to ask for work, or are you

waiting for work to come bowing down to you? — living for weeks on what you're going to get some time."

" Get your ax, we want every man jack able to walk," the foreman replied, slapping his gauntlets together.

On his way into the yard he asked: " What's your name, young man? "

Jussi was not sure at first which young man the foreman meant. To make sure he asked: " Whose name? " The foreman took him by the arm and said: " Not whose, yours."

So much ceremony confused Jussi: young man — and then to have to say his name out loud.

" Jussi, ay, but your surname? "

A new problem. Jussi had never had any use for a surname and wasn't even quite sure whether it didn't mean a second Christian name.

" What's your place called? " asked the foreman.

Jussi cast a look around him and said: " Toivola."

And so Jussi, after having first been Jussi Nikila and then Jussi Tuorila, became Johan Toivola. Under that name he began his first exciting day as a real wage-earner. Difficulties cropped up at once. Jussi had no gauntlets; he had to get them from the foreman's storekeeper as an advance on his wages. He had no trimming-ax and no hewing-ax. The first day seemed endless; the thought kept on recurring to him that back of everything he had no better home to go to than Toivola.

Winter wore on towards Christmas, and work in the forest settled into its normal grooves. Most of the men still lived in the new cabin, which because of the church glass used in its windows had been dubbed the " Temple." In the evenings cards were played there and usually there was a terrific hubbub. Peddlers found their way to the Temple, and already it was being rumored that girls were visiting the place. Jussi slept in the old cabin with the older and steadier men. He was still suffering from a nameless sense of helplessness. Mina kept up the nagging manner she had first adopted when the men came, and snapped at everybody, but Jussi she appeared to hate. Jussi was Isak's chum at the tree-felling. Isak took charge of their joint earnings, and on the first two pay-days Jussi never even saw his wages. He was given his food at Toivola, but nothing had been said about what he was to pay for it. He guessed that his earnings were the same as Isak's, and Isak had plenty of money, and so had Gustav, who had become a driver. Jussi once affected surprise at this state of things to Gustav.

" Isak's won at cards," retorted Gustav with the air of an expert. Gustav had adopted from the outset an attitude of cold superiority in his dealings with Jussi. He seemed entirely to have forgotten the night of the celebration at Tuorila, and whenever Jussi tried to approach him in a fellow-adventurer spirit, he turned surly. Now, too, when Jussi complained about his lack of money, he said:

" What do you want money for? Do you think

Mother's not going to charge you anything for all that time she was keeping you? "

" Yes, but your lot got twenty marks from my uncle," ventured Jussi, who was beginning to feel aggrieved.

But at that Gustav snarled with a new venom: " What are you talking about, hey? "

The whole forest with the working gang, the foreman, and everything seemed to be ranged behind Gustav. And Jussi was alone against them all, in peril of being thrashed.

A playful fellow, that foreman. He hardly ever said anything out straight in a serious voice. But this joking manner of his was a mask behind which he hid other traits of character — traits that were difficult to define, but which were certainly lacking in those under his orders. Hard to say what they were — all one knew was that he was the boss and the others the gang. The men were familiar enough with him, but were they to attempt to find out which of them was most intimate with him, they would have been baffled. They might conceivably have discovered that no one really knew the boss intimately.

The person who prided herself on knowing him best was Mina Toivola; no one answered him back so boldly as Mina. Keinonen saw through Mina, and Mina was convinced that she saw through Keinonen. But in one matter Mina carried on as it were a private game outside of Keinonen's sphere; and perhaps she really fancied that she was a whit sharper than Keinonen. For which reason Keinonen in his own good time blandly spoiled Mina's hand.

Keinonen had noticed on one occasion that Jussi had no money, although pay-day was only just behind and Jussi had had no opportunity of spending his money.

" Don't you know there's a rule in these forests that a man's got to have money on him? " he said to Jussi with playful severity. And when pay-day came round again, he gave each man his money separately instead of paying them in pairs, as they worked.

" It'll save you the trouble of sharing it," he explained.

Jussi saw his wages for the first time — more than seven marks.

But that evening when Jussi arrived at the cabin there was storm in the air. Isak had hurried home before him. Isak and Gustav were sitting at table, and Jussi made for his usual place beside them; the formality of invitations had been dispensed with long ago. But no spoon had been set for him, and when he asked for one, Mina said, controlling herself:

" Them as has their own money finds their own spoons."

Jussi went to the shelf to fetch himself a spoon, whereupon Mina, in an outburst of fury, struck him on the hand with a ladle.

" A devilish pack of trouble all of a sudden," she screeched, " when a woman has to be watching her property every second to see it's safe; let me tell you . . ."

That was only the beginning of a deluge, the chief contents of which were that Jussi had been fed for many a long week after he had been kicked out by his employers as a good-for-nothing rogue, and not a penny had he paid all that time — and so on. Keinonen was in his jolliest mood when he came into the house in the middle of it and in his pleasantest Savo dialect began to lay the ground for Mina's thorough discomfiture.

" What's Mammy's own little boy been doing now to make his mammy so cross? " was his first sly question. And having, by his own methods, reduced Mina's flow of language to gasps, he proceeded to find out how long the young man had been at Toivola. Then he asked how much Jussi was supposed to be paying per day.

" I charge him what I see fit, and that's my business, and I say nobody's going to play the judge in this shack," Mina retorted.

The men exchanged sly smiles, as though in their opinion Keinonen was getting the worst of it.

" Now, don't start reminding us about shacks," said Keinonen silkily. " Don't you remember how quickly we got that other shack into shape? Why, we could put together another shack like it from the ground up in a jiffy." And Keinonen went on to say that Mina could charge the young man at the same rate as she was charging him, and asked Jussi how much he had paid so far. Jussi explained that two of his pay-days had gone to the family and that Mina had already been given twenty marks by his uncle. . . . But at that Mina exploded, and this new explosion was even more terrific than the previous one; she screamed, shook, and wept. Even Keinonen blushed, and it was in a voice that this gang had never heard him use before that he at last thundered:

" If you don't stop that lip, there's going to be real trouble for you to rave about."

An angry silence was the result. Keinonen turned slowly on his heel and cast a stern, all-embracing look on the other occupants of the room, though no one had whispered a word.

There had never been, and never was to be again, any other occasion in Jussi's life when justice was so amply meted out to him. The upshot of the affair was that Jussi was allowed to keep his present wages, and Keinonen promised to see that Mina henceforward got her due. He also promised to look into that matter of the twenty marks. Mina was crestfallen; her helpless rage found its only vent in snorts and a cautious slamming of objects. But Jussi was thereafter to sleep in the Temple.

In the yard Jussi fingered the down that was beginning to grow on his face and listened to the noises made by the horses and the murmur of talk from the men. For the first time in his life he had money of his own in his pocket; it was wrapped up in a rag, and his hand kept on straying to it. Standing there alone, he sensed the power behind the forest works. Forest work — the idea behind the words led somewhere upward, to gentlemen of ever increasing might and importance; there was money there, so much money that there was no end to it. There was something scaring, something almost overpowering, in being in touch with the source of money in this way. Money was a queer thing; it seemed to lay vague demands on him.

He crossed over to the Temple, where he was to sleep that night. Card-games and a cheerful medley of voices were uppermost in the impression made on him by the room. Tomorrow is Sunday and we shall all be going together to church. The coming day of rest tends to make the men good-natured and lazily playful. Men from different parts of the country tell one another ghost stories and adventures with wolves. The talk gradually flickers and dies down until one of the men begins his regular evening fabrication of astounding lies, spurred on to ever new efforts of invention by the half-bawdy comments of the others. Someone recalls the row to which Jussi had given rise in the other cabin, and for a little while he is the butt of humorous remarks. Jussi takes their jokes stiffly, a little surlily, but no one is sufficiently interested in him to start baiting him in earnest. Jussi is felt to be an overgrown lad, too soft yet for this crowd.

At last the men begin to drop down on the straw. The prevailing mood is unusually gentle this Saturday night. The married men think of their earnings and of what they are going to do with them when they are safely settled down at home again, the young men think of tomorrow's journey to church. The spirit of the forest gang has found its romantic pitch.

Jussi thinks of his altered relations with Mina Toivola and of his homeless state. He remembers his mother as she was when they set out together for Tuorila. He even dwells in memory on the night of her death, which stands out solitary, apart from every other moment of time in the picture of life that has formed in his mind. Do tears still rise to his eyes?

To Jussi it seemed that his trust in Keinonen's good-will had been premature and exaggerated. When, having foolishly lost his money at cards to the other men, he demanded, almost tearfully, his money back, Keinonen no longer resorted to his authority on Jussi's behalf, but joined in the jokes cut at his expense. So that was what the world was like after all: in the last resort you found yourself alone. Jussi gradually forgot his sentimental evening dreams of his mother and of former days on Pig Hill and at Nikila. Already winter was on the wane; the sleigh-tracks had a watery gleam and the felled pines spread a scent of spring. On his departure from Tuorila the earth had been bare; the winter that had then loomed so largely before him, too long for his thoughts even to attempt to range to what lay beyond it, was now retreating. What particular part of the time that lay behind him had been the endless-seeming winter envisaged by him?

On the ice, booms were already being linked together to enclose the rafts of logs. The weeks lost their settled atmosphere of hard continuous labor; the floating season was drawing near, Tuorila would soon be left standing here with its master and mistress and the money they had received. Of the magnificent trees only the stumps and tops, branches and bark-shavings were left in the forest, always in the same order, so that they formed on the surface of the earth a lightly sketched picture of the fate that had befallen the vanished trees. After days of increasing light the hour came at last when in the Toivola Temple only a moveless stuffy air remained of all the winter's happenings. On that sunny day even Mina could not help feeling a vague melancholy.

Most of the forest-cutters applied for floating work, among them Jussi — Johan Toivola. He bought, acting on his own in perfect liberty, a new pair of top-boots and, still acting for himself, began to procure his food from the houses in the villages along the floating channels. A growing sense of manhood filled his mind. There was dignity in the feeling, but at the same time it weighed a little on his spirits. The money he possessed made him feel restless; it was as though it was always silently demanding to be used for something.

Slowly the great raft crossed the broads along the south-western watercourse, making for the river Kokemäenjoki. On the pontoon a fire burned constantly under a coffee-pot and in the shelter of the hut the men played cards. The horse plodded on its eternal circuit round the windlass. Beside it Keinonen greases his boots.

" Baptist, hurry along now! " calls out the man whose turn it is with Jussi to row ashore for food. A ducking had caused someone to refer to Jussi as John the Baptist, and thereafter that, shortened to Baptist, has been his name on the raft. Should a newcomer, on being regaled with tales about the shrew Mina at Toivola, ask who the woman was, the answer is: " See Baptist over there? She's his mother."

Jussi goes ashore, to a different farm again today. His experience is constantly broadening. The relations between men and women, of which his knowledge had gained little in exactitude since his Pig Hill days, become thoroughly clear to him during the course of this floating season. He gets drunk and experiences for the first time that peculiarly human state which invariably manages to combine two wholly contrasting elements.

Life is broad and outwardly carefree, yet at bottom a vague sense of shelterlessness persists. When this ends, where then?

Even after the floating season was over, Jussi was not turned adrift. He stayed on as one of Keinonen's men. In the forests now in the market the trees had to be counted before it was safe to buy them, for here and there farmers had already begun to set such stiff prices on their forests that it would have been unwise to close with them in the old fashion. Jussi thus became one of the counters, and by the time that job was finished, the lumbering season was soon under way; the Satakunta forests were being well bled. The break with the old, of which starving sowers had dreamed in the fine spring of 1868, was now being realized, and — as commonly happens in such cases — in a manner very unlike the dream.

Jussi grew up to manhood during the years he was a "company's" man. Chance had made him a wandering worker, though he never really grew used to the part. After the first year was over and he was again felling trees, with a forest cabin for camp, he already knew the ins and outs of a lumberman's life, and the following years did little to develop him. He would willingly have taken a hiring as a farm-hand, only the locality was everywhere strange to him and he had no wish to return to the neighborhood of Tuorila. Reserved though he had become by nature, he felt himself drawn, ever since those Toivola days, to his present familiar circle because his companions never all changed at the same time. Whenever his thoughts now turned in the evenings to the past, they invariably ended up at his early days at Toivola before work in the forest had begun; and he thought of them as of a peril from which he had unwittingly been saved. He had actually to reassure himself that he need never go back there, that there really was no forgotten circumstance that might yet compel him to return to that state. He had left no debts behind him, taken nothing away with him — or had he? No — they had no claim on him whatever.

His Tuorila days lay already so far behind that his thoughts now never reached so far. A picture of the house might suddenly form in his mind, but it awakened no response in him. The master, mistress, and children at Tuorila were farther removed from him than anything else, almost as though they had never existed. Those times and those conditions — the standing around in the bakery, the clean bed — they had been wiped off the slate of his mind. Life began from the moment of his arrival at Toivola, and the entire contents of his present existence lay in the fact that he need never return there.

Until even this mood became rare.

At the age of twenty-one he was of medium height, a slightly bow-legged, gray-complexioned man with square-cut hair. In a crowd he tended to disappear; no one bothered for long to make him a target for jokes. Many live the most intensive years of their life during their wander-years, piling up adventures which they later — after time has gilded them — never weary of relating. Not so with Jussi. In his moments of rest he would be conscious that the raft was now floating down such-and-such waters and that the houses on the banks were now so-and-so. At the most he might remember where he had been last year at this time and note his own full acquaintance with a lumberman's job. Around him were men of many kinds. Some went ashore on mysterious errands of their own. Jussi was incapable of going anywhere on his own. There were girls ashore, but somehow they all seemed to be older than he was. He did not know how to behave with girls, except in his private longings. He could not even talk bawdy about them as smoothly as the other men, let alone steal into their attics on his own initiative as he knew some of his companions did.

Somehow the summers passed. And in those summers were moments of such beauty that although Jussi was not especially sensitive to beauty, he could not help being affected by them. On one lovely Trinity Sunday morning a steamer — a fireboat — passed the raft, bound from town on a country run, with a band on board playing lustily a tune familiar to all from their childhood. A faint tremor of agitation and devoutness passed through the men's minds; here and there a man hummed weirdly distorted words, the meaning of which he neither understood nor felt any need to understand.

For the moment all were solemn and moved. Keinonen said: " Now, boys, all in the same uniform and off to church! "

The company's stock of clothes was in the same boat as the other stores. Each of the men was given a red coat, white trousers, a shiny belt, and a peaked cap; then quickly into the boats and off towards the soft greenery of the churchyard. Only an old sickly cotter, the owner of the horse, was left on the raft. The steamer had already disappeared behind the tiny headland before the boats were half-way there. Jussi was at one of the oars. The moment was richly harmonious; the lands and forests seemed to be trying to indicate that the nation was living through its happiest years in their spirit. Along the thousands of lake shores waves plashed their secret message, to which, somewhere in this corner of the country, a great gentle-hearted poet was listening. The red-coated men who were now landing from their boat did not know what a poet was, but the message of the waves penetrated with childish ease to their subconscious minds. They were company's men, capable of cursing fluently; yet the crust was very thin over the soft and pure unspoiled souls admired by the poet each time he happened to pass near men of their kind.

A spirit of exaltation surged through Jussi's mind as well, as he stood up or bowed his neck in church with the others. The elevated atmosphere of the church eased the inexplicable inward strain under which his torpid life had lain during the past years, a strain which he had consciously recognized only as a vague feeling of being exposed. What years had accumulated, a single moment might brush away. The church was full of worshippers who had come from their own homes and could look forward to a comfortable Sunday afternoon in their own yards. The singing and the Word of God that billowed so freely in the sunny air of the church seemed to be reaching out to these people and the yards awaiting them. In this place Keinonen seemed to shrink and lose his power. His choicest witticism would here be as nothing against the tinkle that arose each time the sexton

changed the numbers on his black gilt-framed board and
then turned it round again for the congregation to see.
The red coats were part of Keinonen, and Jussi, for one,
was ashamed of his own coat. It made him feel as though
he were being forced to speak Keinonen's funny dialect.

Along such paths as these Jussi's thoughts wandered
all through the sermon. He remembered the sickly old
cotter left behind on the pontoon, remembered him as
he looked when he thrust his wages into a leather bag,
notes and coins all mixed up together. Solemn as it was
in church, the old cotter seemed to be nearer to Jussi
than Keinonen and the red-coated lumbermen. The
cotter was of those who go from church to their homes,
of those who have hymn-books and handkerchiefs.

The sermon was a long one, and Jussi had time to become lost in a dream that he too would soon be going
home to a church-day breakfast of gruel and potato stew.
Nowhere does the human imagination, even the stiffest-
jointed, roam with such ease as in church at sermon-
time on a summer day. It grated on Jussi's sensibilities
to have to go back to his boat when the service was over.
There was no help for it, he had to go, but the trip to
church marked for him a change in the inward contents
of the summer.

In the autumn Keinonen took his men into the parish
where Jussi had come into the world; Jussi even helped
to count the fine untouched timber in the forests belonging to his birthplace, Nikila. Many, indeed, were

the forests he had tramped with Keinonen since their
first association at distant Tuorila. But now it happened
that one morning Keinonen failed to awake. No one
had seen him die; in his death there was the same touch
of mystery as in his life.

The work was then nearly finished, and by the time
the new boss arrived the men were ready to depart, for it
was early yet for the cutting to begin in that district.
Jussi was the only one to stay on; his explanation was
that he would wait for the winter work to begin, but he
had a feeling that there would be no more lumbering
for him. Not that he had any definite plans; it only
seemed to him that several circumstances pointed in that
direction. He was twenty-four years old, but among the
lumbermen he still felt himself a mere boy. The state
of mind that had reached its culmination during that
last visit to church had returned again and again, and
it was perhaps under its influence that he had begun to
save money. And when Keinonen died, it was to Jussi
almost like a sign that he, too, had finished with the
gang. Also the coincidence that he had returned to the
place of his birth was not without significance; there were
people still living in the locality whom he recognized,
although they, like the surrounding landscape, had entirely lost the atmosphere of those times before the
famine. Gone were Pa Ollila, Benjamin, the old Nikila
farmhouse, the cabin on Pig Hill. But once he ran
across an old woman who, as she stirred her coffee-pot,

asked him in a moved voice about the manner of Maja's death.

He was an alien in the place, and at first he felt less secure than when he had been a company's man; the way his money melted annoyed him. Yet he could not make up his mind to leave with the other men. Who knows what his real reasons may have been for staying, for everything was totally unlike his dreams on that Trinity Sunday?

The former little Jussi of Nikila became a big farm-hand at Pirjola, a farm near the village where he was born.

The '80s had begun.

THE HEART OF LIFE

WHEN a man returns to his birth-place after roving the earth, he needs to be a better man than those who have stayed at home. One expects of him good clothes, money, and an air of superiority. He has to be a good dancer and a smart fellow with the girls. If he fulfills all these requirements, he is a success. He can find a job as overseer on a farm, a farmer's daughter for wife, a good croft to live on; before he grows too old he buys a farm and by skilfull management succeeds in paying off the mortgage. All this may happen, and has often happened; there is nothing in the existing order to prevent it. Yet how ludicrous the idea of a career of this kind seems in connection with our friend Juha! — in his own parish Jussi has become Juha.

His former home, Nikila, is now the best farm in the village, or at any rate quite the equal of Ollila. The farmhouse where Pa Ollila's son Anton lives with his strong-willed wife is new and imposing. The wife is of proud farming stock and people say that she refused to set her foot in the old stuffy house at Nikila. Nor was she called upon to do so, for at the time when Anton took over the farm, builders were willing to work for their food only; carpenters from the North jostled their way by main force into the job; indeed, they all but fought for a chance to help on the building. For the Ollila clan never ran short of bread; Pa Ollila, watching the walls of his son's house rise from the road, observed: " It's all right so long as your bread and your money lasts."

Before autumn the main building had been completed, the outhouses had been repaired, and a large garden plot cut off from the adjoining field and surrounded with a stout stone fence. The mistress moved in before Christmas. And to those who after that remembered Nikila as it used to be, it was as though Benjamin and his crowd with him had been banished for some shameful reason after having wrongfully occupied the place too long. Life was spacious and clean there now. Not one of the farm-hands had yet seen the mistress in her shift as they might have seen Maja any evening. The elder son went to school in the church village. Benjamin's old untouched forest had now been sold for the first time. The former disreputable Nikila had become one of the solidest farms in the locality.

Beside such matters Juha's adventures out in the world paled to insignificance. Obviously he could expect nothing better than a job at Pirjola as man-of-all-work. Pirjola was a small old-fashioned farm; he was the only farm-hand. There was one maid.

One Sunday afternoon Juha set off along the highway, making instinctively towards Harjakangas village to see all these changes. He had on his new creaky top-boots; in his pocket he had over twenty marks. He remembered his age and noted in that connection that he was a full-grown man. The former little Jussi Nikila a man — so time passes. When he saw the improvements in the Nikila yards he thought: " You have altered, but so have I." Old Benjamin had never once come into his mind during the past few years, but now Jussi remembered him, and, strangely enough, he felt sympathy for his dead father. As he walked past Nikila towards Ollila, his gait and the expression on his face unconsciously reflected something of old Benjamin's arrogance. A faint defiance vibrated within him as he thought of the present owners of Nikila and Ollila. " Men like them lording it here and selling forests; little they know of lumbering. We've seen forests like these before, we have " — and the Nikila forest once belonged to Benjamin, Juha's father. " And then this fellow goes and sells it as though it was his." As Jussi strode on, he almost looked as though he had recently sold the Nikila forest. The knowledge that he had money in his pocket was a source of unspeakable satisfaction to him. No one can guess, merely looking at a man, how much money that man may have in his pocket.

Juha did not return from his walk until late, and when he retraced his journey he was a little drunk. Between Ollila and Nikila he attempted a yell: " Ollila skinflints! " He was Benjamin Nikila's son, and don't you forget it. But he did not yell loudly; he heard the sound only in his own brain, in his consciousness, which the drink seemed somehow to have stripped naked; it seemed to be looking on from inside him as he strode forward deep in admiration of his father, Benjamin. It looked on and would not be driven away. " Ay, these were once Benjamin's forests, but he has lost them beyond recall. That may anger you, but it all happened in perfectly legal fashion. Walking about and telling yourself you're the son of the man who owned the farm and forests and that you — yah! — Look you, this is a different farm now, it's got nothing at all to do with your father, it's Anton Ollila's farm, understand? Anton is his father's son, Pa Ollila's, who came from Kokemäki. That's the way you've got to look at matters, and then you're on the right track. You're going now to the Pirjola living-room to sleep, but don't forget! — you've got over twenty marks in your pocket. Go ahead with your think-ing from that point. Look at other people, see how they live in the world that's around you."

So the consciousness that was behind his intoxication went on, though it used no words.

And Juha, who used to be Jussi, went to bed in the Pirjola living-room that Sunday night and on many fol-lowing Sunday and week-day nights. He was a quiet farm-hand, whose family circumstances were all known to the older people in these parts; the stock he came from was revealed clearly enough in his smallish eyes, in which those who knew could detect a hint of old Benjamin, though the man's nature certainly resembled more that of his mother Maja. He was queer in some ways, but not enough for him to be specially talked about for that reason. Thus, he had an odd way with money. He took out his wages to the last penny, which made the master regard him as a spendthrift. But Juha no longer wasted his money; he only wanted to have his money in his own possession. It was not thrift, for a thrifty farm-hand abstains from taking out his wages as long as possible.

He stayed one year at Pirjola. His companion in service was a maid well on in years, who left at the end of the year to get married. "It depends on the farm whether a maid finds a husband or not," declared the master of Pirjola, and he repeated this remark a couple of years later when Juha — then back again at Pirjola — was fixed to marry the maid Rina, also in service at Pirjola.

The most intensive inward experiences of a farm-hand or farm-maid invariably occur between a Sunday afternoon and Monday morning. The time in question is for persons of their status a fateful period sown with pitfalls. The fleeting sense of liberty is then at its height, expanding as the evening wears on, until during the night the demands and proper proportions of life within the social framework are liable to be wholly forgotten.

Many an unrecorded fate has taken a decisive turn on the night before Monday morning. That night has been

the treacherously fascinating portal to a life of hardships, the gateway to marriage, and a subsequent grind-
ing in the mill of reality. And in that mill no trace remains of the sweetness of a past Sunday night. It means
days of hard work and nights of killing frost, sick children
and a wife grown careless and flabby, looking on whom
one no longer remembers what she looked like when she
was a girl — girl indeed, can the word ever have applied
to a creature of her appearance? It means the loss of children and cows, leaking huts, and arrears of work. It
means everything except moments of harmony, for in
the jaws of that mill no one loves his or her nearest. The
rare moments in a cottage yard on Sunday mornings,
still in shirt-sleeves, these are too insignificant to count
much. Even at such moments nothing is so distant and
unreal as the Sunday night on which it all began. It is
always a melancholy sight to see a farm-hand and maid
gravely attempting to imitate something which, if it is
to succeed at all, calls for quite different qualifications.

Juha ought to have had experience enough of the
treacherousness of Sunday afternoon's spell of liberty.
Had it not once at Tuorila led to a shameful beating?
But the common property of all vice is that at the decisive
moment it compels its victim to forget altogether the consequences of previous indulgence, and the vice of enjoying to the full one's liberty is no exception.

One could indeed hardly expect a person at Juha's
stage of development to extract wisdom from hidings
and Monday morning wearinesses and then take that wis-

dom for guide. Every Sunday evening, especially in summer, he set out to roam the village. He went to dances,
although even the polka was too difficult for him. Sometimes he became a party to a mild spree. Nothing serious
happened to him on such occasions. He was often present when a fight started, but was never among the
victims. He was cautious about buying drink; for some
reason he was afraid to club money with others for the
purchase of liquor. Again, it was not thrift; he was only
afraid of the responsibility incurred. But as he was
never any trouble to anyone, he was often given drinks.

Nothing happened to Juha on his Sunday evening
outings. Or so it seemed. Perhaps fate had shown
greater cunning than usual in its disposition of the consequences of these outings. One outing had after all
quite decisive consequences which later, as decade gave
way to decade, led his hitherto fairly colorless life into
channels where in its own inwardness it strikingly re-
flects a certain side of human life.

Although Juha on these solitary outings of his affected
to regard himself as a person of some wisdom and worldly
experience, he was annoyingly aware of one great de-
ficiency in himself: he was still without experience of
any kind in regard to women. In company he acted
otherwise; he would slowly unfold a knowing coarse
remark and give well-disposed married women an opportunity to say: " Juha's not so soft as to let any woman
hook him."

Juha enjoyed unspeakably remarks of this kind and

acted with increased assurance the part of one who has had enough of that sort of thing. But when he returned to his lonely bed and heard Rina, the maid, breathing on the other side of the fireplace, that was another matter. He had never touched a woman, there was the rub. And although Rina was no better than she should be, Juha would have given anything to be bold enough to steal across the living-room to Rina's bed. One night, when a dead silence on the other side of the fireplace made it seem likely that Rina was awake, Juha crept in her direction, coughing as he crept, only to find that she was not in her bed. He stretched himself out in the empty bed and lingered there awhile. But when Rina returned home from the village, Juha was already back in his own bed, pretending to be asleep.

Rina was two-and-twenty, a girl lacking in ballast and loose-natured. She did not come from these parts; the master had hired her at market partly out of a sense of humor when she asked him for a job. She did her work apathetically and ran away at night as often as she dared. Young men were afraid to venture into the Pirjola living-room at night, but so far as Rina was concerned, there was no need for them to do so. The strangeness of the locality was no hindrance to Rina even on her first Sunday night. She sang in a whinnying voice her own country dance-tunes in the living-room, to vanish later into the village, whence she returned some time after midnight. Circumstances alone made her the object of Juha's secret dreams. She did not seem to take any interest in Juha; she whinnied her songs to herself and on being addressed by him gave any careless answer. But Juha's imagination went on working.

The fateful Sunday night came at the turn of July — harvest-time. Juha's sense of being alive was at its height that evening; it accumulated so many new shades that from Juha's subconscious mind the wordless question kept on floating up: " Is this I? Am I living the fullness of my manhood? "

That evening he drank liquor for which he paid; together with two other men he bought a jugful. Then, drunk, to a dance. And there it befell that a man seized Juha by the lapels of his coat, and Juha thrust the man on his back on to a bed. It was only play; nevertheless the marvel had occurred that Juha had laid another man on his back. On his way out Juha made grabs at the girls in the dark porch, and as he puffed homewards alone towards Pirjola, the emotion uppermost in his mind was a strong conviction that he had long been the equal of anybody in this neighborhood — for that matter, of anyone else anywhere.

He entered the dim living-room and went boldly to see whether Rina was at home. Not yet, said the empty bed. Juha moved cautiously to the window and remained standing there. His brain did nothing of its own volition, but seemed merely to gaze on whatever was brought before it. In quick flashes there appeared to it the inward visage of intoxication and even of the secret well-spring of all life, but too rapidly for Juha to grasp them. From his body came messages of a faint nausea, but his soul refused to accept them.

Along the twilit path came Rina, escorted by two men. Behind his intoxication Juha found pleasure in the thought that those men would not come into the living-room, but Rina would. Juha remained beside the window until Rina opened the door. Then he made towards Rina.

For the first time in his life Johan Benjamin's-son, at the age of twenty-six, holds the whole of a woman in his arms. He does it under the shelter of his drunkenness and the previous experiences of the day; again his body acts on its own, automatically, his brain merely notes what happens. The whole being of the man is loosened from the fixed past and floats in air. The woman offers little resistance; she is fatalistically slack. At last she says:

" What's put so much life in the old ram all of a sudden? "

To Juha her words are bliss. They form as it were a firm resting-place for his being, which is now so strangely afloat.

But when, later, he is back in his own bed, his intoxication has faded. He experiences one of the deepest disappointments a man, even a better man than he, ever finds befall him. He is overwhelmed by a torpid emptiness; nevertheless life and the world turn an entirely new face on him as they watch him lying there. One brief event has again as it were gathered up all the countless little events of the past farm-hand years and welded them into one whole; he has reached a new platform on the path of his life, whether higher or lower than the one preceding it matters little. Before sleep comes to him, he has already perhaps seen himself in a coming part as the man in a little cabin. At this stage such fancies can still be pleasing enough.

It was a significant coincidence that Juha's advances came at such an opportune moment for the maid Rina. Such perfectly dovetailing coincidences do occur in life. Rina was absolutely without home ties of any kind and had further good reason to suspect that she was with child by a man who she knew would never marry her. For although it has sometimes happened that the heir to a farm has married a maid, Rina knew well enough that she was not the kind of maid of whom farmwives are made, least of all after matters had fallen out as they had. Her attitude towards Juha had hitherto been non-committal; there were thus none of those hidden antipathies which in cases of this kind occasionally lead to talk of a woman's martyrdom. Rina went to dances as before, but was wholly faithful to her Juha. A touch of brazenness had crept into her behavior, as though to meet in advance any gossip that might arise about her.

After what had happened marriage was to Juha something axiomatic that needed no further consideration. The whole of his inward life, and in part also his outward actions, were conditioned by that fact. A pleasant anxiety took possession of him when he made plans and estimates for the future. His henceforward nightly visits to Rina at the far side of the fireplace were only a minor detail that had to be looked after along with business of greater importance. For him Rina was wholly and solely the woman he was to marry. He knew nothing about Rina's circumstances or birth — they had been married some months when an old woman like a blackbird, whom Juha rightly took to be Rina's mother, paid a visit to them — and as they lay side by side they never spoke to each other of marriage. What was there to speak about? Juha tended to be absentminded and Rina fatalistic, and no agitating scenes took place between the two.

Juha did his work rather more carefully than usual. The master, who was keen-scented, was soon aware how matters stood, and being a good judge of character and a juror at the circuit court, was content to bide his time. By adroit manipulation, however, he once led Juha to take up the matter of his own accord, and once the subject had been broached, it was thrashed out to the end. The master found out how Juha stood as regards money and heard his plans. Juha was hoping for a crofter's holding on Pirjola land.

The master looked quietly elsewhere as though thinking it over. In reality he had no need to think the plan over even for a moment. He saw before him Juha, Rina, and the money, three things that at the moment were childishly begging for recognition as an admirable and promising foundation for an independent existence, but whose inherent insufficiency for the part the aged farmer saw with relentless clarity. Goodwill, pity, and aversion blended in his attitude towards the matter, but he would not be a party to it. He therefore gave no definite answer to Juha's hints about a croft, but displayed all the more sympathy for and interest in the coming marriage. He gave Juha a few paternal, manly words of advice, with the result that Juha was in no wise downcast by the interview, but on the contrary let his hopes soar ever higher. During the rest of his life Juha retained the warmest feelings for the old master of Pirjola. Later on, when the master was already invalided by old age, Juha would sometimes turn to him in his difficulties and invariably met with such overflowing friendliness that the actual object of his visit might remain unspoken. Juha's life was on an upward grade the whole of the time he was at Pirjola — right to his wedding, the entire cost of which was borne by the master.

It was Rina who first mentioned the word " marriage," speaking in a familiar bad-tempered voice and letting slip offhand how matters were with her. There ought not to have been anything unexpected in that, yet Juha felt the agonized sweat break out on his brow. There was little of the bold lumberman in Juha that evening. His thoughts hammered away at possible and impossible ideas all at the same time. The question of marriage was suddenly fraught with entirely new meaning; now it really was inevitable, and it had to be accomplished

within a definite space of time. Where to go to live?
Pay rent to live in a corner of somebody else's room —
that was a terrifying thought. Even if the master were
to stake off a cotter's holding for him, there wouldn't
be time to build even a three-walled hut. His money
wouldn't stretch to anything like the total sum needed,
and he was himself incapable of shaping the logs for the
walls of a house. Juha gasped and twisted in Rina's
bed. Rina merely lay still in an indolent attitude as
though she were enjoying Juha's perturbation.

In the daytime Juha worked harder than ever, as
though trying in that way to keep his dreams of a croft
alive, although as the time grew shorter his chances of
obtaining one shrank. Rina's condition was by now obvious to all and tended to arouse queerly unpleasant
moods in Juha. Something alien seemed to be drawing
nearer to him, something with which he could feel
no connection whatever, but which notwithstanding
reached out towards him. In Juha's mind there was
never at any time the slightest definite doubt about the
child's paternity, nor did this side of the matter ever
get beyond the whispering stage even among the village
women; as soon as Juha and Rina had settled down in
their new home it was forgotten altogether. Nevertheless, to Juha this first child remained a mysterious
stranger, and Rina was constantly falling out with him
over it, often for no apparent reason whatever.

They became cotters, not on Pirjola land, but on a
farm called Yrjola. At the last minute, after the banns

had already been put up, the master gave his final answer.

"I have no land suited to a cotter's needs," he told Juha, "and, for that matter, you're not in a position to build a cottage just now. But you go and speak to old man Yrjola, he's got that Krapsala place lying fallow, a big cabin and a nice bit of land — you've only to move in. The buildings are in repair and I think he'll have you." Pirjola was not arousing vain hopes in Juha; he had already in all secrecy arranged the matter.

So one Sunday Juha spent several hours in old man Yrjola's room. Old man Yrjola champed away in proper farmer style, coughed and went every now and then to his pipe-shelf to refill his pipe. He did not offer Juha a smoke. Juha's cheeks burned and he rubbed his perspiring palms together. A bargain of a kind was struck. As Juha was unable to take over all the land attached to the croft, no contract was drawn up.

"You can stay on there as long as I live, anyhow, provided you live decently and do your work," Yrjola promised.

Until further notice Juha was to do a day's work a week on the farm for rent, finding his own food.

Feelings of liberation and of being inextricably bound for life struggled for the upper hand in Juha's mind on his way home to Pirjola. A hundred hands seemed to be stretching out for his small savings. Well, he was bettering himself, that was one comfort.

The master and Rina were in the house when Juha returned with his news, and all three thus found them-

selves together. The moment seemed somehow to ac-
quire a vague solemnity, which the master lightened by
announcing in an optimistic tone that he would pay for
the wedding, seeing that his maids would go and get
married.

"You, Juha, have been a faithful servant," he said,
"and if you keep on like that on your own land, the
Lord will bless you." And the master put an end to the
meeting by remarking jokingly: "As a crow flaps from
one field to another, so you, Juha and Rina, now flap
from Pirjola to Yrjola."

A feeling of inward satisfaction was reflected in the
master's every movement.

Soon after that the wedding was held in the Pirjola
living-room. In the excitement of that event nearly
everything that had existed so far was drowned; all that
was not drowned was Rina's blessed state. It obtruded
itself from hour to hour, even as the excitement was
dying down. In the yard a fight of no small dimensions
developed between the uninvited, but of this the bride-
groom knew nothing; he had fallen asleep drunk on the
bed in the bakery. The man slept, but his ears were
open and through them violin notes emerging from the
hubbub entered his dream-consciousness and kept up
there an exceptional continuous state of bliss such as
was never to visit him in waking hours, never again even
in his dreams.

Meanwhile Rina collected over thirty marks in wedding gifts as the night wore on — twice as much as the previous maid at Pirjola had got. She even went out into the yard to quell the fighters; the boldest of these followed her into the house to dance and contributed many marks to her dowry.

The croft was some distance away in the middle of the forest attached to the Yrjola farm. It had lain un-inhabited for a long time and was so thoroughly decayed that in ordinary conversation no one remembered its real name. It was referred to as Krapsala, but even a stranger could tell by the sound of the word that that was not its real name. Its latest occupants had been rather a funny lot and had caused the place to be so nicknamed. After Juha and Rina had moved in, the place began to be called, after its new occupier, Toivola. Only the master, when teasing Juha for being late or for other omissions, would address him as the master of Krapsala.

The young couple moved into their new home in the week of All Saints' Day. The weather and the state of the track were well adapted to dispel any illusions Juha may have been harboring; Juha got a glimpse of what was henceforward to be his day-a-week road at its most characteristic. The wheels of the cart sank in places to the hubs, and the horses strained with outstretched neck and agonized glance as though afraid it was going to sink into the earth.

The couple's entire worldly possessions were on the cart. There was Juha's cupboard — his dream during his Tuorila days — and Rina's chest with its gaudy North Finland pattern of posies. There was a bedstead that had lain ten years under a storeroom at Pirjola, but now displayed gleaming white bottom-boards; it had cost a silver mark, with a sheaf of straw thrown in for a bargain. There was a makeshift tub, a bucket, and a milk-pail, an iron caldron on feet, a stone bowl, and four wooden spoons; Juha's household goods thus included some things beyond what was absolutely necessary. All this property had been accumulated in an atmosphere of mild excitement. In the load were also the raw materials a cotter couple setting up on their own would need for their daily food; these included five pounds of pickled sprats, twenty pounds of hard bread, a sack of potatoes, and two pounds of salt. The whole lot had been bought with money of which Juha had just so much left that he was sure of being able to pay the carter. The beginning was thus not unpromising, for countless households have been set up in Finland on a smaller material foundation and succeeded remarkably well.

Nor can it be said that the couple lacked that inward aliveness which in enterprises of this kind is the main thing. In their voices rang a poorly veiled challenge as they kept up a running conversation with the carter. Rina, in particular, emptied her whole stock of farm-maid witticisms as she toiled on beside the others, her big belly bouncing alarmingly as she jumped over the worst mud-holes. And at last they saw their destination, a group of gray board-roofed buildings in the midst of a melancholy swampy wood. They drew nearer and nearer, until at last the cart stopped in front of an unprotected door-opening. And then — in with the baggage! But now it became apparent how thoughtless Juha had been: he had gathered fuel into stacks in the forest, but had forgotten to bring even an armful to the house; the carter very nearly had to set off homeward without a drop of coffee. Luckily there were the remains of an old fence lying about. With some difficulty a fire was finally lit with the aid of these. The pale day showed by then symptoms of dusk.

After the carter had gone, the heavy stillness of the decaying building penetrated into the married couple's ears with the effect of a stunning noise. Rina felt inclined to weep when visions of her recent carefree servant days came into her mind. So this was where the path of her life had led her! Juha moved around, seeing at every step a terrifying number of things to be done. Every time he remembered their stock of food a tremor ran through him. The food would last so-and-so long — what then? In mid-winter there would be little work even on the big farms.

So began the married life of the couple, acquiring before long all its characteristic little features. It dyed the whole of their existence, took visible shape in their clothes and the way these hung on them; it showed in the permanent expressions on their faces, in the man's beard and the woman's hair, in the way they sat or stood.

Christmas had not yet come when Rina went for the first time in Juha's absence to the village to barter bread for coffee. Not a day went by without differences of opinion, and sometimes they quarreled; it was the substance of their daily life, that which gave to each day its own faint individuality, but much more a strong rigid sameness.

On occasion Juha went to work on the farms in the village, and when he returned with his scanty wages in his pocket he was especially irritable. He had supped at the farm where he had been working and it was therefore not seemly to eat a second time at home, hungry as he was. He drank coffee and nagged at Rina for neglecting to do this or that. Rina, however, had her blessed state to fall back on; secure in this, she let herself go slack from the beginning, with the result that slackness became habitual with her. For when the child came, there was plenty to do looking after it, and by the time it was a little older, there was a second child on the way, bringing with it the same right to take things easy and let the housework slide.

For a time Life seemed to be considering what it was going to do with this married couple. It pondered the matter up to Christmas and then decided to let them rise a little in the world, seeing that they were still beginners who imagined that their road led upward. Lumbering, which has showered such blessings on all classes in Finland, came once more to Juha's aid. Forest-cutting began at a site three miles away, and Juha worked there steadily for two months. He was there when Rina, entirely alone, gave birth to her first child, a boy who was later christened Kalle Johannes.

When he came home that evening Juha got such a shock that he never even gave a thought to the early arrival of the child. Then, seeing that there was no cause for anxiety, he recovered from the shock, but it left behind a curious sense of emptiness, the nature of which he never understood. It seemed to him that something invisible had brought him up with a jerk and demanded to know: " Who are you? " " I have a child now as well to feed," came into Juha's mind — and again a powerful momentary agitation shook him. He thought again of money, of which he now had a little, but not nearly enough for all his needs.

The flat winter day waned to a quivering twilight and then it was night. In the Toivola living-room lay three people who that night instinctively drew apart from each other. Even the child did not want to suck; every now and then it wailed.

That February night, however, was only one of those solitary moments when even an undeveloped soul moves uneasily in its prison. Life kept to its decision and let the Toivola family climb a little way towards prosperity. News of this good fortune filtered through at last to old man Yrjola, to whom Juha had so far only vaguely hinted how things were going with him. The master heard that there was a cow at Toivola — to be sure, not Juha's own cow, but a borrowed one —

and a horse that was all Juha's own, a wretched crock bought at Easter market. About the cow the master knew already, having given permission for it to graze in return for an extra fifteen days of Juha's services at the farm, but when he mentioned the horse to Juha, he was told that grazing rights had been arranged for it with someone else. Thinking the matter over, however, the master began to entertain his own suspicions, and one day when summer was at its fairest he was seen to set off towards Toivola. In spite of his weak chest he was going to see how matters stood on the croft.

The master did not go straight to the house, but turned off the track before reaching the gate and came to the edge of the fields at a point in the forest where he could not easily be detected from the house. The panting old man cursed with quite youthful vigor when he saw what his crofter's game was.

"So that's the way we're getting on in the world, stealing a tow from somebody else's boat!" he muttered to himself.

It was not only anger the old man felt; there was something else in his mind that aroused a curious combative spirit in him. He seemed to scent a cunning attempt on Juha's part to raise himself to terms of equality with him: "So that's it, is it? Well, we'll see!"

Juha had well over an acre in cultivation, although they had agreed on a much smaller patch. And his barley seemed to be thriving wonderfully well, although the

land had lain fallow so long. Must have been an old
dunghill somewhere left by that former tenant. But
then the master's glance fell on Juha's new fence, and he
was uncertain whether to laugh or curse. A new split-
wood fence stretched across the field, cutting off the
sown part from the fallow. Posts, rails, and bindings
from the best stand of spruce near by! And beyond the
fence, on the old field, a horse standing peacefully beside the resting cow. So that was his grazing rented
from some other fellow! Invigorated by anger, the master set off towards the yard.

In the house terror reigned. Juha's eyes were like
two gray buttons, and Rina began a hasty attempt to
tidy the room when the master was already coming up
the yard. The master noted the alarm caused by his appearance and was somewhat mollified. He held forth
sternly nevertheless for some time and at first let Juha
and Rina come to the conclusion that they would have
to go. He showed, meanwhile, no signs of hurry — a
favorable sign, that. And at last he sat down on the steps
and began to speak in another tone. Now that Juha had
a horse and the beginnings of a cow, he might as well
take over the whole croft in return for, let us say, so-and-
so many days' work for man and horse, so many days
without the horse, so many days helping with such-and-
such tasks, and — the master reeled off the quantity of
berries and how many milkpails and tubs Juha was to
bring and how much flax Rina was to spin. . . .

1 4 7

The day that had threatened to end so disastrously became almost a festival day. Before leaving, the master even came into the house and accepted a drop of coffee. And after he had gone a still, uplifted atmosphere reigned long in the living-room. Juha was to work his way upward to the status of a " big crofter," almost the equal of a poor farmer.

It had not entered Juha's head to criticize the master's terms. Not after the shock he had had. What he had to do now was to start on the nearest job; he would move that fence, to begin with. Silly it had been of him to put it there. The master had grounds enough for cursing him.

Juha had become a big crofter; soon people were addressing him as Janne.

One summer Sunday Janne — who used to be Juha, and before that Jussi — sat in his shirt-sleeves in the yard, day-dreaming of a general improvement in his circumstances. These seemed to him to be in the nature of a disease. He gazed on the bulging corner of the house, thinking hard. In the end he had to admit to himself that as long as he lived he would never know what it was to live in a new house. His hair was falling out, his teeth secretly crumbling. His wife was inside the house, and his children. There would be more and more children yet. Yes, the house was in a bad state, but it wasn't worth while troubling to ask the master for timber for a new one. And there would be the builders to pay.

Every single joint would have to be shaped by a carpenter. One of the touchiest spots in Janne's hide was his ignorance of carpentry; it was one of the basic hidden weaknesses of his life.

But what if he were to pull down the old shanty and try to put it up again on a smaller scale? The master wouldn't object to that, seeing there would be no need to draw on the forest for new timber. At the same time it would be an improvement and would help him to get on better terms with the master. " I'll earn money in the winter hauling paper. . . . Lucky I didn't sell the horse; the money would be gone by now, and where should I be then? Things have got to start going a bit better, ay, and the wife'll have to be taught something. All she does is play about with the brats, and everything is always as upside down as it can be when I come home."

Janne set off slowly towards the pasturage. His dawning hopefulness made him want to see the horse that was to haul paper for him next winter. There it stood beside the gate, lean, sulkily swishing its tail at the flies. It favored him with an evil wink, as much as to say: " Well, here I am, go on with your plans."

There is his horse and there is the house, and in the house a family life that goes on from day to day, through good times and bad. No stopping it, no getting rid of it. Every time a new child comes into the world, the stream of that life broadens, and Janne has to keep up with it. The farm and the master and the fact that he has not a shred of a written contract are all part of it. A series

of forces which, in spite of their being seemingly opposed
to each other, minute by minute pulled something onward somewhere.

The rye was ripening. It ought by rights to have been
cut this Sunday afternoon, for he will have to be at the
farm all tomorrow and the day after, but in Janne's
mind is a curious apathy. It won't be falling yet by
Wednesday and he can start in the morning then.
Always best to begin a job in the morning and get properly down to it.

Half past two in the morning. The dawn is red on
the north-east horizon, but it is an hour yet to daylight.
In the Toivola living-room the wife is asleep, snoring
with her mouth open, and the children, in pairs, are also
asleep; one sees naked little buttocks and arms. Janne
alone is awake. He moves warily so as not to wake the
family. He curses in a suppressed hiss when he holds
his milk-flask to his nose. Unwashed since he last used
it, it gives forth a sickening reek. He looks again at
the sleeping woman. He had again forgotten to tell her
last night to wash it, and without telling she would of
course never remember a thing like that. Janne smiles
a crooked weary smile and goes to fill his flask. The
funnel is missing, and how is he to fill a flask from a
pail without a funnel? He is out of the living-room now
and can swear freely. Using a soiled coffee-cup, he labori-
ously fills the flask.

Next, bread into his knapsack. Against his will Janne

is compelled to admit that the store of bread has shrunk too quickly; some of the loaves have walked off without waiting to be eaten. Everything slips through his fingers; his angry protests might just as well have never been made, for all the effect they have. "There she snores in the house with her brats and here am I off to the reaping for the master. Where's my sickle now? — wants sharpening of course — have to grind it at the farm." As he crosses the yard, Janne sees the funnel on the ground where the children usually play; but that is the last of his trials this morning in his own home. He strides along the morning-damp track, finding satisfaction in the thought that the tool he has to carry is no heavier this time. From this distance his feelings towards the house he has just left are almost friendly. His day-dreams begin; always on these early morning walks to the farm pleasant ideas come into his head.

Work begins at four and his walk takes an hour. To-day he has to bestir himself a little because his sickle needs sharpening. It turns out, however, that the master, on an important day like this, has rung the bell a quarter of an hour earlier than usual, and when Janne arrives the men are already off to work. The master stands in the yard, a treacly smile on his face.

"The master of Krapsala likes to sleep, I see, with his wife on the hem of his shirt. That's why he's never on time."

The master says his say, coughs, and turns aside. Janne takes his food-bag to the porch and hurries after the others; his sickle is still unsharpened and he tries to give it a rub with a whetstone as he walks.

Abuses were undoubtedly rife in the crofter system as practiced in Finland in those days. Janne, to be sure, does not yet know the meaning of the word "abuse"; he merely toils and grouses. On this very day he had scarcely worked five hours before it came on to rain, and rained hard enough for the master to say: "We'll have to stop reaping now. Come tomorrow if it's fine."

Unwillingly the crofters and other day-laborers took their food-bags and slouched off in the rain, each to his own home, to quarrel viciously the rest of the day with their wives and children. And lo! the next day was fine. Again the same long tramp with milk-flask, food-bag, and sickle — and four hours' reaping, after which the rain came down and the same walk home along slippery roads was before the men. A working-day meant fifteen hours at that time, and in two days the men had thus done nine. Towards the end of the week the weather turned really fine and the crofters' own rye began to fall while the men worked on the farm. Sunday had to be devoted to their own crops. Those who had planned to attend Communion service had to put off their church-going to the autumn, annoying as it was when one thought what the roads would be like then.

What the roads really were like one found out when the time came round for the autumn plowing. On those occasions Janne need not get up earlier than three, but it was a job to find his brown horse in the dark; a white horse would have been better. For when the brown horse happened to stand quite still, so that not the faintest clank came from its bell, the only guide to where it was standing was to listen for its sigh. Then there was the bad road before him, with the wheels sinking in up to their hubs. On the cart was the plow, a pair of shafts, and food. It was a troublesome load, always tending in the worst parts of the road to slide off the cart.

A plowing-day was the hardest kind of work, especially for the horse. The master was in the fields most of the time; he had learned by experience during the course of time that a crofter's hanging sheath-knife didn't swing very often when the master was away. And the example set by the crofters made the farm-hands take things easy as well. The master walked about the fields stick in hand, coughing in the damp air. He watched Janne Toivola cursing and yelling as he jerked at the bit of his horse. But he suspected that the fury was mostly acting, and when the horse, panting and stretching its lips, next stopped, he gave it a sounding thwack with his stick. And the horse moved all right. The longer the day wore on, the oftener the master had to brandish his stick at it, and even then when evening came it was a good bit behind the master's own horses. Trying, these crofter-days, especially the man-and-horse days, to master and men alike.

A few of the crofters tried to save all that early morning bother by coming to the farm with everything they needed the evening before. But that was no use to Janne.

He had tried it once when he had to be at the farm at two in the morning for the flax-braking, but he had not slept a wink, and at half past twelve he got up in a rage, moved the hands of the clock forward to two, and then woke up the other men. Even the strongest strive vainly against the laws of nature, and in Janne's case nature seemed to have decreed that he was not to fall asleep except in his own home with Rina beside him. In spite of all the friction of married life, the nagging and squabbling, one thing still happened every night: before going to sleep Janne laid his arm round Rina's neck. He laid it there and patted her a few times on the shoulder, gave her a squeeze, and patted her again — there, there! Astoundingly he did that, and then went to sleep. And so he never went a second time to the farm for the night, but preferred even on flax-days to get up at one, take the heavy flax-brake on his shoulder, and in pitch darkness struggle along the muddy track.

Flax-days were among the most exhausting of the days he had to labor for the master. Nearly always a competition would spring up to see who could brake most flax, and that went on from two in the morning to daylight; a dram of liquor was the only refreshment one got all that time. Then came breakfast, and after that the men went into the forest to gather stakes until it was too dark to see.

That was how people worked in Finland during those happiest decades in the nation's history when the march of material and spiritual progress was at its fastest even among this lowly people, who feared God and sincerely loved their great and kind ruler.

Janne Toivola carried out his plan to earn money in the winter by freighting paper. He earned money; coming home from a two days' journey, he might have more than ten marks in his bag. Paper had not yielded the whole of that sum; part of it came from the sale of butter. But the money had one curious property: you never knew where it went. Hard to say whether the family were any better off than before. But the drawbacks attendant on freighting were obvious enough, although Janne tried not to see them. The horse grew thin and lazy, so that whenever he had to put in a day's work on the farm, the master's stick played on its ribs whatever the nature of the work. The manure tended to get left in the cow-house, and the cow had to be dried with straw, no one having had time to cut spruce twigs.

That was how it worked out, but the prospect of another ten marks sent Janne on ever new freighting trips. Ever frequenter became those early risings when Janne went off to Tampere, and late nights when he returned. Someone invented a new nickname, Paper Janne, for him after his horse had been seen nearly twice a week over a long period outside the Kuuskoski paper warehouse. And when anything happened to be needed round where Janne lived, the usual remark came to be: " We'll have to go to Toivola. Janne'll fetch it from Tampere next time he goes."

But then came a fateful freighting trip.

Janne had bought two and a half quarts of spirits in town, and the pint was for himself. The weather was cold, his feet and hands were freezing, the horse was white with rime. Half-way home Janne took his first drink, and from then onward the proverb about giving the Devil an inch came true. Janne was drunk by the time he reached his own neighborhood and dropped in at the house where he was to leave the two quarts. Seeing that Janne had started his spree, the others joined him, and Janne was in no hurry. He stayed at his neighbor's until close upon midnight, quarreling occasionally and making friends again. But during one quarrel the woman of the house taunted Janne with Rina's secret sales of bread. Janne had of course had his own suspicions about this, but now he felt deeply insulted and, at a loss how to crush his sharp-tongued hostess, he was casting about him for a suitable retort when he saw his neighbor's watch hanging on the window-frame and arrogantly offered to buy it. The neighbor was willing enough, provided they could agree about the price, and eventually a bargain was struck and Janne left the house with the watch and little more than a mark in his pocket. But within him raged the spirit of old Benjamin Nikila.

Grunting to himself he drove into the yard, unharnessed the horse, and then — then went into the house. The family was asleep. Janne lit the lamp and spoke in a low but menacing voice.

" So that's what we're doing here — sleeping! "

He took off his coat — no one woke up. He took off his waistcoat and struck the floor with it with all his might.

" Up, you rascals! " he bellowed.

Rina, Kalle, and Hilda bounced up as though something had hit them, and they were near to being hit, for Janne had seized a billet of wood from the fireplace and was running round the room shouting and cursing. Only half-dressed, the wife and children sought refuge in the wintry night. Such a scene had never occurred in the family before.

Janne raved in the living-room, alone. But not altogether alone; in the bed, motionless, lay little Ville, usually the liveliest of them all. There is something strange in the fact that he does not move; Janne goes nearer, his intoxication evaporating. The boy screams, but does not move.

" Did I hurt you just now? "

No answer, only a trembling look.

Janne feels unhappy and bewildered; he stares around him and sees his waistcoat and fragments of the watch on the floor. He stoops down to look: yes, the watch is in bits. Janne remembers everything and collapses. He has been hauling paper to Tampere and this is his homecoming.

His rage vanished and gave way to a stupid numbness. Rina and the children stole into the room, stiff with cold and weeping. Kalle looked more scared than the others. But the father took no notice of him; he sat quite still,

157

staring fixedly before him. Then he fell into a doze, but managed to get to bed unaided and was soon asleep.

What a time! Rina heaved a trembling, tearful sigh. Janne was still ignorant of what had taken place while he was away; there was something else behind his outburst. Rina pulled on her frock and went out to see what had become of the horse and sleigh. On her way out she caught Kalle's furtive eye. It was Kalle who had hit Ville on the back with a rail yesterday and probably crippled the child. A wave of disgust and pain surged through Rina's bosom; clearer than ever before she had caught, a moment ago, a glimpse of Kalle's father, his real father, in the boy's face. A dull bitterness, wholly lacking in any redeeming element, gnawed at Rina's heart.

Life went on, but again on a new plane. The next morning Janne ought to have been at the farm with his horse. But the horse was unfit for work, and his own state was not much better. The work-day went to swell Janne's arrears. Janne drove manure from the byre into the yard, for by now the cow's back almost reached the ceiling. No manure had been carted into the field this year because of the freighting trips. And the net yield from Janne's freighting was now a little more than a mark in cash — and bits of a watch on the living-room floor. And Ville was in bed with an injured spine.

The day was miserable beyond words. The unhappy parents could not even scold one another, each having his own load of guilt. Kalle's life, however, was henceforward made so unbearable that Rina secretly found employment for him at the far side of the village. And that was the last of Kalle at home. Hilda, a pale, silent girl, was thereafter the oldest child. But Rina was with child again, and soon there was a second girl, Lempi. Then came a boy, Marti. More and more children.

In circumstances like those of Janne and Rina matters rarely come to a decisive crisis as in better situated families. All that happens is a series of small jerks which jolt the course of life as it were from one step to another. After each successive jerk no one troubles to dwell much on what has happened; one submits to life on the new plane. For, after all, life is life in all its forms, and the only absolute in relation to it is that it has to be lived.

Ville at first recovered to some extent from his injury. He moved his limbs, ate, and slept. But then his spine began to ache again and finally to fester. By that time the agitating events of the period when Ville received his injury had long ago been forgotten. The family merely existed in a general atmosphere of decay. Out of sheer apathy thoughtless acts were committed such as the sale of the horse.

So the years went on and grew into decades.

The curve of Juha Toivola's life — the reversion to the name Juha marked a public recognition of his decline to his former status — curved gently downward; the slightly firmer attitude towards life of his middle years had relaxed. Viewing his present existence with a strictly neutral eye, one seems already to divine in it that atmosphere of a long-drawn deep sigh which precedes a well-earned slumber. But while one's limbs ache, sleep refuses to come; one may heave many such sighs before one's head finally droops to earth. There is time for one to grow bitter and calm down again more than once before the great liberating sleep descends on one.

Juha sold his horse, and the money was soon spent. The last of it went to the druggist for Ville's medicines, a few copper coins in change was all that remained. Weeks of man-and-horse days were in arrears, and for that matter Juha had so far only done twelve other workdays, and half the summer was gone. Juha tried to get the master to believe that he had not yet succeeded in finding a horse to his liking. The master listened without remark.

Old Yrjola had died. The present master was his son David, who had been to a farmers' school. He was known to have said that the old man's agreements were not binding on him; he was not bound to recognize them unless he liked. The farm was his by purchase from the other heirs and he saw no clauses about crofts in the deeds. That was when he first became master; nevertheless, up to now he had " recognized " all of his crofters as such.

But what is going to happen to old Toivola with all those arrears of work?

The day is a windless Sunday, the time three o'clock in the afternoon. Juha Toivola sits on the threshold of his house in his shirt-sleeves, bare-headed and unshod. Outwardly he feels warm and comfortable, and matters are nearly as well with him inwardly. He can't always be dwelling on how he is going to get a horse, and he cannot yet prevail on himself to admit that it is practically certain he will never again have a horse of his own. Life is at a standstill, as before a change of wind. A meekly mild old man's state of mind not far removed from tears.

Through the open door Ville can be heard moaning at intervals. Rina asks him whether he wants a drink. Something to moisten his lips, that is all that can be done for him. It is long since he last ate any food. The medicines gave out some time ago. They were useless, but now that the end is drawing near, it would be a relief to have something to give the child. Sad that there is no medicine in the house. One can only moisten the boy's lips, a service he accepts humbly each time.

The longer Juha sits there, the more frequent grow the moans and the offers of a drink. No recollection of the cause of this misery — Kalle, now out in the world — ever enters Juha's mind, even by accident. At the moment Juha is not even angry with Rina. Rina is slack, but she bears this cross without complaint.

A softened grief induces a curious state of harmony in Juha's thoughts. The languid perfection of the day takes on something of the same color as these thoughts, and when he now thinks of horses, he does so dispassionately. Ville's moaning takes on the form of a benediction on this particular problem; it is as though Ville were begging for a horse. Ville's sufferings seem somehow to justify his claim to a horse.

Juha rises to his feet. He has no intention of doing anything about the horse; he just pulls on his boots and coat and sets off for a walk. Nevertheless he keeps a steady course towards the village and at last admits to himself that he is on his way to Pirjola. He will decide when he gets there whether to take up the subject with his former master or not. He might run across the master somewhere outside and so be able to chat naturally about other things should he feel shy about mentioning the horse.

The old master of Pirjola does happen to be in his tobacco patch, and they talk quite comfortably about one thing and another. The old man even asks in a gentle voice how the boy is getting on — not at peace yet? No, not yet.

"Ah, there's a child who's being tried longer than most."

The old man goes in, saying: "Won't you come in for a smoke?"

"I don't think I will, I've got to be going a bit farther," answers Juha, swallowing hard.

And he walks on, having decided nothing. His body with all its five senses moves along the twisting road, but his mind takes no part in this forward movement. And so, that Sunday evening, he finds himself entering a house more alien to him than any other house in the parish could be. He enters the new house at Nikila. And

once he is under an alien roof he has to tell his story, or
the people, finding him errandless, might think he had
gone mad. He explains his plight to Anton Ollila, now a
middle-aged man. And Anton, on his part, does not appear to be disagreeably moved. Anton's voice, when he
speaks, is as strident as though he were shouting to the
stable-hand to tell him which set of harness to take. Juha
tells in his heartiest tone the story of Ville's sufferings; he
describes the high cost of medicines and his other
troubles. Finally Anton says:

"To speak out straight, I know quite exactly that I'd
never see a penny of my money again, and I'm not the
man to throw my money down a well."

He moves youthfully about the room as though looking for something, and then goes out. Juha, too, gets up
and leaves and is not in the least downcast. But he no
longer has the courage to go through the kitchen. He
sidles out through the big porch, whose many small
window-panes set up an angry tinkle when he opens
the door. When he has crossed the yard and reached the
road, he feels free and safe again. What a long walk he
seems to be taking this evening! The air has cooled and
become suffused with a faint glow after the long, happy
day.

The corn is in the ear in the villages, and when he is
in the woods again, the grass-tufted ground smells moist.
On such a ramble even the most miserable human being
cannot keep his thoughts fixed wholly on everyday matters. Juha does not think of the coming week's labors;

he even forgets to think about the horse. Around him hovers the glamorous mood of a calm summer night, in which tiny memories of remote incidents on the path of his life seem to be embedded. An unnatural presentiment of happiness casts its deceptive spell over him. At home, sleep reigns in the living-room; Ville, too, has found rest on his ragged couch. Rina half wakes up when Juha stretches himself out beside her, but falls asleep again at once; she has to make the best of the hours when Ville is asleep.

Blessed be the Finnish summer night. After Nature has thoroughly subdued a man by turning on him her week-day aspect for decades, prodded and jerked him along the bewildering uphill and downhill path of his life, she will on some summer night withdraw from his aging consciousness her day-time goads and let it sink into the moist peace of her dreaming landscape.

The visit to Nikila had only served to swell Juha's curious mood. Nothing would have been harder for him just now than to let his thoughts dwell on work and new efforts. Happiness was on the way along some other path, not through them. Ville breathed audibly in his bed; Juha did not hope that he would die, yet he did not believe the boy would get well; it was not that. . . . For hours Juha was unable to sleep; he did not even try. And at last his thoughts took a definite direction. He would not go a second time to Pirjola, nor to Nikila; he would go to Tuorila, on the far side of Tampere. Why, he had relatives there. He did not think in terms of the price of a horse or anything as clear-cut as that, but simply that he now had to go there — this summer. After his mind had made this discovery, it grew calm. He got up from the bed and in his shirt went to the doorway, but soon came back as though afraid the night sky might tamper with his ripened decision. Then he slept.

But in the morning, when he awoke, he actually set off on his long journey. He described life at Tuorila to Rina and hinted mysteriously that he would not return empty-handed from his visit. Rina muttered something about work-days, the sick child, and other such matters, but finally relapsed into indifference, and Juha was able to embark on his sleep-walker's expedition, from which he did not wake until he was at Tuorila.

It was a strange prelude to the new phase through which long-suffering Juha was still to pass.

Juha's uncle K. Tuorila had died a highly respected farmer and left behind him on the farm a spirit of enlightened progress with which the visit of nondescript Juha was wholly incompatible. The estate was being administered by the heirs. The young master soon recognized Juha and carried him off from the kitchen to the parlor by way of the main entrance. Just at that moment the telephone rang in the hall, an instrument Juha had never seen before at such close quarters. A sturdy young gentleman, the master's brother, came to answer the call. He spoke Finnish sure enough, but Juha understood nothing of what he was saying, although he overheard every word, the door being open. ". . . folk-poems . . . Vepses. . . ."

" Tell him to drop in here," shouted the master from the parlor.

Juha found himself most of the time in the company of that same young gentleman, who was very friendly. Only he would go on pressing Juha for folk-poems, whatever they were. " Folk-story " he dimly understood and was sorely worried because for the life of him he couldn't think of a good yarn, damned if he could. Instead he let his tongue glide over to his domestic circumstances, and the young gentleman listened, saying every now and then: " Is that so? " Finally he gave Juha ten marks and led him to the room where a bed had been made for him. He then went away with a " Good night."

" The same hope here," answered Juha.

Juha was left alone in the room, in staggeringly fresh air and a tremendous clean smell. Against the background of this cleanness Juha's journey began to take on the complexion of a fantastic affair in the planning of which he had had no part. Juha inspected the curious system of sheets in which he was to lie. The sheets were of thin, remarkably white linen, and there were two of them, the top one unaccountably entangled with the blanket. Juha disengaged it and spread it under him, remembered the ten marks he had been given, and stretched himself out on the bed.

From somewhere very far away he seemed to hear Ville's moaning, so clearly that it was only after a moment or two that he realized how impossible the idea was. A sudden woeful longing swept over him. His mind awoke from its long delusion, but his weary body fell asleep in the midst of an overwhelming cleanness.

DEATH DOES ITS BEST

THE AUGUST day is long and sultry. The true nature of such a day is best apprehended on a fifteen-mile heath that lies between two parishes and is pierced by a winding road known since time immemorial as the North Road.

On this road generation after generation of solitary travelers have felt the terror of the wilderness stir faintly in their blood; driving home from town in their carts, with befogged glance turned inwards, they have, as one long mile succeeded another, gazed critically at their own childish fundamental selves stripped naked by alcohol, reviewed their past and planned their future, and ultimately, as the first village came into view, roared their relief. In the middle stretches of the heath even the smallest rises have names well known three parishes away, so often have they enabled travelers to estimate the distance they have covered, so often, driving up them at a walk, have men paused in their thoughts to wonder how matters are at home and grown secretly humble under the weight of the great unknown. On each side of the road spreads a pine forest of unchanging height and appearance; somehow, it is hard to imagine that anyone owns these forests. No birds sing in them, no hares start up. At one spot someone has attempted a tiny holding and may possibly have lived there, but not for long. The boards nailed over the windows are gray with age.

Only gadflies escort the traveler from parish to parish in the summer, whirling round the heated horse the whole way.

Noon has come. At a certain point on the heath road Juha Toivola sits at the wayside, overcome by the heat. He has been to Tuorila; today is the third day since he left there, and he is no farther than this. He has made slow progress. He spent one night at Tampere in the waiting-room of one of the shopkeepers; he bought a loaf in the market-place in the morning and has eaten that. He also bought a pound of coffee and the same quantity of sugar, and in his bag he still has eight marks, a five-penni coin, and three pennis. He still has that much left of the money given him at Tuorila. The problem of how best to spend it weighs on his mind. A drink would have tasted fine, but he lacked the courage to walk into the shop where they sold liquor. Those marks were the fruit of his high quest and therefore trebly valuable. They burned and stung him. At home a score of matters awaited him for which the money ought to be used; for most of them it wasn't enough. It wouldn't

buy him a horse, for that matter — a horse — hm. That
train of thought always ended now in a bitter smile.

In the deep silence of the heath Juha gave free rein
to his decision. No need here to snap at anybody and
pretend to have mysterious plans. He is drawing near
to his own parish after a long journey — the day after
tomorrow it will be a full week since he set out — and the
mood of such homecomings is always vaguely melancholy, whatever kind of failure the journey may have
been. Especially if the journey has been a fiasco does an
old man feel inclined to tears when he approaches his
familiar, wretched home. And Juha Toivola is an old
man. He senses that this journey, the longest he has undertaken for decades, has been as it were a treacherous
threshold on the other side of which the step is so deep
that taking it one comes down with an unpleasant jar. It
has jarred Juha into old age. He feels that as he sits by
the wayside on his return from the place where, his
childhood at an end, he saw his mother die.

Old age has come to him, and one of its allies, the
demon of self-examination, now for the first time really
holds defenseless Juha in its iron claws. The five days'
journey is like an epitome of the strivings and aims of
his whole life; it seems to move away from him to a distance to allow him to see it clearly, and to it lead all the
thousands and thousands of little circumstances in his
life that at bottom were none of them really favorable.
There are so many of them that when, as at this moment,
they all try to enter his mind together, his body instinc-

tively recoils and would fain be on the move again, as so often before. But on this occasion the demon is stubborn. " You are tired, the day is hot, and at home awaits you, you know what; so sit where you are, visitor of relatives."

Remembering the childish hopefulness of his departure, Juha spat. Another work-day in arrears for this week; how many are there already in arrears? His man-and-horse days are in arrears since the spring; " I sold the horse, yes, I really did that." And only now does the truth penetrate crashingly right to the bottom of his mind, that he will never have another horse. All that is left of the price of the horse are the three copper pennis at the bottom of his bag.

In direct sequence come new thoughts of growing bitterness: " Rina — I married her that time — the very same woman — I have lived with her all these years and slept my nights beside her. . . ." The idea of Rina surges into Juha's consciousness like a brand new tremendous truth . . . he sees all Rina's ugly traits as a stupendous irreparable fact to which he has unaccountably become fettered. Rina does not depend on him, nor he on Rina; side by side they hang on to life. Along invisible channels, as the years have passed, they have unawares sucked into themselves the sour substance of the other; when they quarrel, it is with themselves they quarrel. Every summer they go together to Holy Communion; they cannot sleep except under the same coverlet, with no words left to exchange, coughing, turning, and sighing.

In Juha's withered brain the natural phenomenon, the process known as the formation of a philosophy of life, dimly emerges. The thin, bald-headed fellow could easier, much easier, learn to fly than to understand those words and their connotations; yet at the given time the actual process takes place inside him as autumn leaves drop from a tree though the tree knows nothing of the botanical process involved. Juha believes that he sees clearly now what life is. It is like some sour, silly substance of which every human being was given more than he could handle, so that he was always in a state of semi-exhaustion, always on the point of being suffocated by it; it was like being put to work in an enormous hayloft with dozens of carts bringing in hay at a gallop. Until at last one died. . . .

The thought of death sent Juha bounding up from the roadside and set him moving homeward at a good pace. He is an old man, fifty years old; in what manner and when will he die? He cannot accept the idea of a breakdown in all the multitudinous combinations formed by him and his family and all the great and small circumstances appertaining thereto since — when? — the beginning of things, so all-embracing they are. Why, the combinations are identical with the world. Other people, those who live and die around him, they are but circumstances belonging to the combinations. " And yet I must die. What is a last moment like? " God? Ah, there was the gap where God came in. " Now I understand God. He will see to it that my death passes off smoothly; He will somehow so square up things that this incomprehensible, stupid, great, and essential world or life will not break up when I die."

Impossible to interpret the primitive movements of Juha's mind in words. He is returning alone from his foolish visit, so utterly incomprehensible to the owners of Tuorila — from a journey at whose goal the wings of his secret canny purpose were scorched to nothingness. And as he walks on, alone with his thoughts, he is stubbornly aware of being at the center of the life he now understands, as he is always at the center of the bowl of sky above him. He is alone, and the world is around him; the day is curiously like a mixture of Sunday and week-day when, dead-beat and hopeless, he finds himself plodding at last through familiar scenes. His very home wears a new aspect, as though it, too, had been thinking things over while he was away. Perhaps there is a little bread left in the house; anyway, one can get quite a lot of bread for eight marks. Home at last. Queerly strange it seems.

One last exertion and Juha ascends the two steps to the porch, passes through the anteroom, opens the door, and feels the familiar smell of rotting wood in his nostrils. Rina is seated on the back bench working at a strange white cloth and makes no remark — greetings are not a habit between members of the family. There is no sign of Ville.

The unfamiliar aspect of the room helps to strengthen an impression that began already in the yard. Ville has

died while he was away. Juha hangs his dogskin knapsack on its nail beside the door. " Which of us two is going to speak first? " The children, too, are silent. After
many questions, which seem to hide under their surface
a nervous irritation, the talk begins to draw nearer to the
crucial point, and then the questioning is left entirely
to Juha.

Juha has taken off his boots and coat and sits on the
porch steps as the evening grows cooler. The sensation
of mingled week-day and Sunday persists, but his dawning philosophy of life has been dealt a blow and is totter-
ing. Ville's death is so great a relief that for the time
being he is unable fully to grasp its extent. Can that
sour, silly material of life be beginning to thin out and
grow sweeter in his case, so much so that he may still
hope to emerge from it, as from a sea, to breathe?

The visit to Tuorila began to take on a new color.
Ten marks in six days is not so bad, and the discomfiture
seems a long way back seen from this distance. The boy
will have to be buried — but what then? Ah, there is
still plenty of the old smart in life; it hasn't improved its
ways very much.

In any case death had achieved so much that Juha,
as he sat on the steps, was a little refreshed. One could
hear that from the lusty way in which he bawled at the
smaller children playing in the yard.

The year wore slowly on towards autumn. In the
summery landscape autumn stole already into the lush

greenery of the boggy woods and the melancholy fields of winter rye. One could still work in one's shirt-sleeves, and through the rents in a shirt even an old skin still glowed golden brown. The shaft of a rake felt warm to a sinewy hand, and a warm scent rose from the hillside they heaped beside the house wall. The scent of freshly gathered twigs was cooler. The sturdy nature of the interior cloaked the tiny miseries of the human nest hiding in its midst in warmth, light, and perfume and prevented its odors from becoming too obtrusive. Yet not for a moment did it lose its undercurrent of melancholy. Up to midsummer its aspect as it reached out right to the walls of the dwelling inspired hopes, but before these hopes had time to materialize, a look of memory crept into it. In August, noontide still has an atmosphere of sated richness, but in its light, as it falls on the neck of a crofter's child, on her scanty brown pigtail, the tinge of melancholy is too obvious to be ignored.

Around a forest cabin life in summer follows the same phases as in the open mid-parish spaces. Only here the intensive plowings, seedings, and reapings of the wide lands are as distant, thin echoes. It is the lot, however, of mankind, however weak the individual, eternally to strive. And even the least energetic is not altogether absolved from this duty. As a heavy working season progresses he grows wearier and wearier each evening, and as the years pass, his weariness increases summer by summer.

A death is a refreshing event. After Ville's death life at Toivola was for long half in the nature of a festival. In the midst of the hardest toil it was as though Juha had to be continually looking back at the years and decades behind — and the past, no matter what it was like, always has a faint halo of sanctity. Juha seemed to be more morose because he spoke less. The hair that still fringed his neck seemed to bristle more and more, and in his little eyes was a strange brittle, stern look. He tried once again to work regularly on the farm. The master let him work and gave up harassing him about the man-and-horse days. And now, when the men rested in the yard after dinner and the debate on any subject grew heated, old Toivola would draw forth God and hold a long lecture in which his view of life as something " sour " was revealed, but in such ranting, accusing accents that the effect on the master and the other men was chilling. Easy to see that Juha Toivola had aged; he had changed a lot that summer.

But it was only the still atmosphere of something solemn persisting in Juha's mind. He had a deep inward conviction that the death in the family had increased his worth, not in the eyes of other men, but in his own eyes and in a way perhaps those of God. He, too, was now one of those who are, as it were, on better terms with God than most, as one among a crowd of workmen may be with the boss and thus have no need to do lip-service or try to curry favor. The great majority of those empty-headed ordinary men had never thought of God except as a name, and for that reason it was right, when occasion arose, to speak out sternly.

When Juha now returns homeward along the familiar fence-side track this late summer, there are no irritating plans fermenting in his head, and he feels no chagrin at the failure of earlier plans. Life since his return home from Tuorila has been, as it were, at a pause, a kind of quiet expectation. To be sure, Ville is already dead, but Juha is clearly aware that his life is still seeking a new direction. There is indeed much to be decided one way or another; something will have to be done about the croft now that he has no horse. Only his thoughts are queerly loath to dwell on that problem. He is grateful to the master each time the subject is allowed to lie. It is as though something else had first to be arranged; but what that something is his mind cannot resolve. He marks time, waiting, from day to day.

Weariness has been a common experience at Toivola for years. Rina was born slack and weak-willed, and a diet of salt water, potatoes, and sour milk had done nothing to steel her character in her mature years. Sitting with child in her lap, she often pondered the nature of the foolish urge that drives a servant to get married, trying in all seriousness to glimpse her motives and catch the moods of those far-off days.

The supreme enchantment of a servant's life is that when you do lie down to sleep there is no need for you to think about what has to be done on the morrow or what has been left undone today. Such questions do not exist for a servant, but for a crofter's wife they are a standing trial. When it comes to children, however, a wife has the better of it. Giving birth to a child is as such what it is, but in a servant's case it means the revelation of her wicked ways, whereas for a wife it is simply part of the general grayness of life, something an outsider views almost with sympathy. And as in that particular respect grayness is and will forever remain a woman's lot, no wonder a servant, too, tries to get married. A mistress's tongue may perhaps help to spur her on — she wants to feel free — but whenever Rina thought of that aspect of the matter she smiled sourly, remembering the unfettered days of her servanthood. It was pleasant to dwell in memory on those days when the old man was away, while waiting for the coffee-pot to boil.

Rina was tired. After her last childbirth something had gone wrong with her, she had developed some feminine complaint that she was ashamed to mention even to other women, let alone Juha. This summer it had become much worse; it wearied and crushed her and often made her feel giddy when she had to pitch hay. The fact that she had to keep it secret gave rise to all sorts of complications. She had to get Juha to sleep by himself. She put the matter to Juha as something she had made up her mind about, crossly and with no further explanation. The husband stared at her and submitted, drawing his own conclusions; the old fellow had himself changed a lot of late.

Harder to bear was the lassitude and a slow ebbing of her strength. She was forced now to leave many essential tasks undone. Ever more frequent became the desire, when Juha was away, to cast herself down on the bed and rest there awhile. Hilda was a very good child indeed at trying, almost as though she had other blood in her veins, but she didn't seem able to get through with the work, for all that she was already confirmed. And you couldn't always be scolding her, a girl like an angel's shadow and not very strong. She had never had to be whipped for naughtiness; if you so much as threatened her she would break into a heart-rending fit of crying, although at her age many girls were running on the sly after boys. Hilda was so delicate and so unsuited to her surroundings that Rina would scarcely have shed a tear if she had died. Often Rina was loath to put the child to work; in spite of her illness she did it herself or put it off for another day.

The summer's tasks have to be done in their proper season. They force even the weary to make an effort. Juha strove, and Rina, too, did what she could. Juha also tried to put in more work on the farm, lest the thought of evicting him should occur once too often to the master. At home he overstrained himself bringing in the grain from the field in a hand-cart and found himself with a shameful rupture that had at all costs to be kept a secret. Life was hard. The summers with their heavy tasks were like a succession of long journeys you were compelled to undertake however tired you might still be after the last stretch. You could not see the end of the journey, nor do you care to spy ahead too often, for there lies death. And nothing else.

One Saturday evening the steam-bath seemed to be sweeter to the body than usual. Sweet it was and there was plenty of steam. But there must have been other deadly fumes hidden in the steam, for when Rina returned from the bath-house she had to take to her bed; it was as much as she could do to put on her shift. She lay speechless in bed, panting for breath, and in the morning she was unable to rise. Rina Toivola was thus really ill. And the next day one might have overheard the following conversation at the crofters' end of the village:

" Rina Toivola's ill, I hear."

" You don't say — since when? "

" Well, she had her bath on Saturday night and got such a pain there that she had a job getting back to the house. Juha was at our place today asking for drops."

" Did he get anything? "

" I'd got some castor oil and heart drops, but you know nothing seems to help against pains in your inside."

The talk then passed to all the different kinds of pains different women in the village had had at various times.

Rina's pain grew steadily worse, and an additional trouble was the delicate nature of her complaint — the countrywoman's ingrained feeling that an illness of this kind was filthy and shameful. Of course, before long it came to the knowledge of the other members of the family. Juha knew now why Rina had made him move to a separate bed. Hilda, too, found out what ailed her mother, yet uppermost in her mind was the memory of the bath night that had made Mother take to her bed. It was from that night she counted the weeks and days her mother's pain had lasted and tried to calculate how soon her mother could be expected to be well again. None of the children had as yet suspected that Mother might die. For the younger children — two-year-old Martin, and Lempi, now going on four — Mother's illness meant the same slightly solemn excitement that Ville's death had brought; Martin possibly felt nothing at all. They were mostly outside in the day-time, and at night Rina's moans failed to wake them.

Juha saw in Rina's illness a sign of something to come. On his trips to the village he would hold forth at length to a few chosen hearers; at home he bustled about in a matter-of-fact way. After bringing home all the " drops " his acquaintances happened to possess and finding that none of them helped, he began to plan a visit to the druggist. The cow gave so much milk that by careful stinting he got together four pounds of butter for a friend to sell in town. The money was insufficient to pay for the medicines, but the druggist, a kind-hearted man, promised to wait for the rest. There was a touch of solemnity in the family atmosphere again when Juha came home from his all-day trip to the druggist's. Lempi and Martin both wanted the pretty paper cap on the bottle, and Rina felt refreshed enough to chide, between gasps, the squabbling children.

Pain was unavoidable, but so were the demands of everyday life. Juha realized that well enough and showed no hesitation in leaving Rina for days in the care of the children, while he went about his business in the village. He had to work oftener on the farm now that he lacked a horse. The small quantity of grain yielded by the field had also to be milled. He had to drag it on a hand-cart now to the village mill; and once there, he had to hang around for hours, for it was the miller's busy season and even farmers tended to quarrel over turns. After such journeys midnight would be near when Juha at last found himself on the forest track, hungry and stopping every now and then to wipe his bald head. In some way, however, the flour on the cart seemed to have achieved a new value, for he could not help the comforting thought coming into his mind that this flour would not start disappearing without his knowledge. At home he would find himself back in the old familiar circumstances — and the smell, which felt doubly bad after a long walk in the fresh night. The children slept on; the parents only glanced at each other, wearily and resignedly, without a word.

The hidden cancer did its work, and the disgusting smell of rotting tissue became ever worse in the room. The smaller children grew more or less used to it when the autumn rains forced them to spend the whole of their time indoors. For Hilda it was worse. Slender of limb and grave as a statue she moved about on the tasks formerly done by her mother. She never conversed with her mother, but simply did as she was told. Rina spoke with difficulty and for that reason asked how the work was going on. It was not always easy for Hilda to understand her broken murmurs; she would sometimes distinguish such words as: " what — do — I — care — Jesus — help me — " The latter words filled Hilda with dread. She stood stock-still, staring with dilated eyes at her mother. Was she going to die? Mother panted again, motionless, her eyes closed. Hilda went to milk the cow with a strange sense weighing on her mind of being far away from her mother. Still an infant at heart, she was being thrust into the part of an adult.

Once when Juha was again away late and the younger children already slept, Hilda dozed off in the dusk on Juha's bed. She dreamed vague tender dreams, hearing meanwhile her mother calling to her. Her heart nearly stopped beating when she awoke and found that Mother was really calling. It was nearly dark in the room; what had happened? She was afraid to answer until Mother called again.

" What? " asked Hilda in distress.

" Light the lamp."

Hilda obeyed, before her eyes the terrible fact that Father was away from home. Mother is dying, and what is to become of them, alone in the forest? Should she arouse Lempi and Martin? She caught a glimpse of their thin faces in the bed before turning to her mother. The woman's agonized expression brought the child to her side. Hilda crossed the room with a sensation of being already alone in the heart of the forest. But Mother was still alive and begging her to do something. Begging her to help, for the first time during the whole course of her illness. . . . Hilda sees all the sorry secrets of the sick woman, feels a damp, warm stench on her face. She felt horribly sick, but experienced at the same time something new, an intimate relationship with her mother, as if she and her mother were of the same age. She noted for the first time the yellow skin and startling leanness that had transformed Mother's expression, making it almost pure. At this moment she would not be afraid even were Mother to die in her hands.

Rina did not die that night. Juha was away so late because he had gone to consult the old master of Pirjola. He had meant to ask the old man for a loan, but the master had guided the conversation so skillfully that Juha was unable to come round to the object of his visit. Instead, the old man listened with great sympathy to his account of Rina's illness and showed no sign of uneasiness any time the name of God crept into the talk. Finally the old master explained in detail the remedy his experience led him to believe was best for Rina's complaint. And Juha was so carried away by gratitude that he almost succeeded in making himself believe that it was for that he had come to consult the old man.

He came home while Hilda was helping her mother.
The unwonted spectacle and the new expression on
Rina's face wakened a conviction at the bottom of his
mind that Rina was past medicines, but all the more
reason was there for him to do something on his part.
He was only doubtful whether to go out at once to search
in the dark for the necessary ingredients or whether to
wait until morning. Rina seemed to calm down; she
closed her eyes and lay still. Juha and Hilda lay down
too, but left the lamp burning.

Nothing untoward happened that night. No sooner
was it daylight than Juha went out to look for his ingredients, which were nothing very remarkable, merely
bird-cherry bark. Of this a strong decoction was to be
brewed and given to the patient when it had sufficiently
cooled. As the liquid was bitter, a little sugar could be
given between sips.

In the morning Rina was so weak that Juha had to hold
her up while she drank the brew. She refused at first to
take it, but by passionate entreaties Juha persuaded her
to swallow three good gulps. It all came up at once, with
such force that it was a marvel the sick woman did not
give up the ghost there and then. A wave of remorse
surged over Juha; it was nearly as though he had uninten-
tionally tortured a little pet animal. That was all he got
for his pains. Rina made a fumbling movement towards
the seat of her trouble, and on raising the coverlet Juha
saw that she had bled profusely. Juha made as though to

do something to help, but the sick woman said in a faint voice: " Never mind." Juha replaced the coverlet.

Those were Rina's last words. After that she relapsed into unconsciousness, though the life did not leave her body until towards evening. In the dilapidated cabin the father and three children waited for hours to see the mother die. Now and again one of them would move away, sit down, and then return to the bedside. At last came the death-rattle. Rina Toivola slept the sleep of death, the woman who during her life had been a bad servant and perhaps a still worse crofter's wife, but who had notwithstanding achieved that exacting position and been given the duty of bringing several new human beings into the world. All her life she had been a negligible person, yet at her death her children sobbed outright.

Even Juha was moved. It brought, somehow, into his mind the death of his own mother in that far-distant locality. The sensation of that alien house cut as with a knife through Juha's memories of his past life, and standing beside his sobbing children he felt that this was his home. Against his will his eyes grew moist and a bright drop trickled on to his nose.

The death of a wife, especially after a long married life, arouses in the husband the feeling that invisible, deep roots are being torn out of his substance. The effect is powerful no matter what the nature of those roots may have been. In very many cases marriage is a heavy

1 8 9

burden on both partners, often an unconscious burden. In the circumstances the death of one of the partners denotes the removal of a burden, and a coarse-minded person takes no pains to hide this. Many, however, experience along with the sense of liberation a deep longing; their mood is one of melancholy happiness. A person of this type tries instinctively to fill the empty spaces left by the roots wrenched out of his being with his or her children; should these take root there is no accompanying sense of burden, but only a pure and light feeling of compensation. That is what happened in Juha Toivola's case.

On the day Rina died and on many succeeding days Juha found existence so mildly harmonious that he had never experienced the like since the night when he became certain that Rina was to be his. He did not bawl at the children, but fussed about with them like a motherly old bird. Now life really was like a holiday. All the problems attaching to Juha's tenancy of the croft had vanished. Just then an eviction would have been a matter of no consequence, an event in the class of the flight of a crow across the field, which Juha had witnessed while a hymn was being sung for the departed soul. The eviction of a man whose wife had just died, leaving behind her little children, would be something uplifting rather than the reverse — it would be the kind of softened fate that arouses no tigerish instincts in neighbors, as a harder fate often does.

The shyness Juha naturally felt in the presence of the master because of those arrears of work was so completely forgotten that it was with the greatest ease he went to tell the master his troubles: he hadn't the money to see his dead wife properly to the grave. And the master gave him the money — Juha had never doubted that he would — how not, to a man whose wife had just died? Everything was turning out splendidly. What better off would he have been if he had got that horse he wanted? A cow was all he really needed; it provided the food they required in addition to bread, and there was now no fear of the bread giving out, with one mouth — and one bread-thief — less in the house. Hilda, too, would doubtless soon be going out somewhere to work. That would leave him alone with only Lempi and Martin. All would be well. The anxiety that had beset Juha that time on the heath road was now far away. He found himself unconsciously humming a hymn-tune.

The change made itself felt in all kinds of little ways. Before, when old women called at Toivola, Juha used to be surly to them, suspecting them of helping to pull down his fortunes; what else did they come for if not to drink coffee and smuggle away bags of grain or flour? Now he had to ask those old women to lay Rina out in her coffin, and he was pleased when they came. At first their expressions were solemn, but when everything was over and the body had been taken to the barn, their tongues began to wag, no more controlling them, and it was a near thing they didn't start marrying off Juha again. After the women had gone Juha felt lonely. If only the burial were over; that was the first thing. . . .

It became ever easier for Juha to adapt his language so as to bring in the word of God. To talk based on the word of God few people can take exception. After Juha had held an auction and sold his sets of harness and other odds and ends, he appeared one Sunday morning in the farm kitchen. He talked for a while with the mistress until the master came and invited him into the parlor, an honor that had not befallen him since his first visit to the farm to arrange about the croft with the former old master. Juha paid back the money he had borrowed. The talk then veered of itself to the subject of the croft. The master remarked stiffly that Juha was quite a large number of work-days in arrears, which Juha in a gentle tone admitted, but pointed out that life had treated him badly this summer in every way. The master agreed and said that he was unwilling to press Juha, but that some arrangement would now have to be made. Horseless as he was, Juha would not be able to farm all the land attached to the croft. Juha was secretly startled and tried to argue that perhaps he would still — somehow. . . .

" You'll never get another horse," said the master, his tone once more stiff. " And you're not much use there anyhow. Bleeding the land dry and stealing forest . . ."

" I've never — without asking leave," stammered Juha.

" When did you get leave to touch that patch beside the far meadow? " The master glared angrily at Juha.

" I haven't."

" I know what I know."

Juha was dumbfounded. The idea of being evicted, coming in this fashion, was terrible. It was clear that the master meant to evict him, talking like that. Juha had never seen the young master look so determined before; he had never heard him use that tone.

The master, meanwhile, had no intention of evicting Juha; he would have been ashamed to do so. Only in some way Juha always got on his nerves and he wanted once for all to put an end to this feeling of hidden irritation. Juha had become too familiar and seemed to be trying in some secret way to get the better of him. Hence the master's unwonted sternness.

The Sunday morning wore on, to the ticking of the clock. Juha sat in the parlor in utmost discomfort as though the place were too hot. When matters gradually began to take a smoother course, Juha's agony changed to a subdued joy, to a cordial agreement with everything the master said. It was settled at last that Juha was to surrender the land at Toivola except for a patch a little bigger than an acre. He could stay on in the cabin, the cow could graze in the forest, and from the fallen timber he was to be entitled to gather a stack twelve feet long every year. In return he was to work thirty days on the farm without his food and another ten days with his

1 9 3

meals. And the day he laid hands on the timber without leave, well, he knew what to expect then.

The farm-hands were at dinner in the kitchen when Juha, his cheeks flaming, went past them on his way home. The funeral over and the matter of the croft settled, Juha was in a hurry to get back to the children and eat his dinner with them.

Cowberry-time had come.

Juha went with Hilda to the family's old favorite berrying-sites, which had often before helped to bring in a little money. How much money berrying used to bring in, it was hard to say, for Juha had always been kept busy at autumn tasks on the land when berrying-time came round and had thus had no opportunity of seeing the money come or the spending of it. This year there was no farm-work to keep him away and Juha plunged with enthusiasm into the fascinating, clean work of gathering and selling berries. Berrying as work is entirely different from the farming of a croft. Each time you empty your can into the big pail, you see at once with a pleasant thrill how the pile grows. And it is all clear profit; no question here of contracts and work-days, no lying up because of snow or rain. Farming a croft and other such back-breaking toil is not really profit at all, only a kind of stuffing to fill in your life, something inseparably bound up with the wife, brats, sickness, and other worries. Juha had had his full share of that; now he feels that he has a chance to earn something. And there are other ways of earning. Too late this year to collect bark, but wait till summer comes again and that, too, will yield a nice bit of money.

The sphere of Juha's activities shrinks, but in shrinking becomes solider and jollier. Three children are left to look after the house when Juha goes off to sell the berries. And soon only Lempi and Martin are at home after Hilda has gone to gather a new lot of berries. Ville has gone, Mother has gone, the hot summer has gone; it is autumn now — au-um, as Martin, prompted by Lempi, repeats. There is a languid stillness in the air; in cabins innumerable the day wears on rayless from morning to eve.

The familiar figure of Juha Toivola can be seen measuring out berries at the door of a villa. A bargain has been struck and Juha wears an important air, for he now knows about how much the berries are going to yield.

The stout lady of the villa watches the berries being measured out and when that is satisfactorily over she gives Juha a note and says: " Haven't you a girl who's past Confirmation age? "

Juha pauses in the middle of the sum he is doing in his head and answers: " Yes, Hilda."

" I thought so. My aunt who married a rector and who's a widow now wants a girl for the housework and she'd sooner have a country girl than one from town, a religious woman like her. Is your girl quiet and steady? "

Juha is still busy with his calculations. He answers

absently, muttering nervously to himself, until he is certain what change to give.

Then, fumbling in his bag, he says: " Hilda's a girl you won't find the likes of anywhere. What did you say your aunt was, miss? "

The day is misty and so still that a cock can be heard crowing on a distant farm. Through the villages Juha tramps the highway towards his home, his basket empty and money in his pocket. Hilda has been promised to the Rector's widow. Ever freer and higher soars Juha's life. Hilda will get on in new surroundings. " My girl is good enough for the gentry to want her. She's sure to find a few pickings for Lempi and Martin. Less and less will be needed to keep the family going, now Hilda is leaving. I can look after the cow myself. It'll be harder those days I have to be at the farm, but we'll manage somehow." Juha began to calculate and plan how he would arrange things now, with everything becoming almost too easy. In the calm moist air he can still hear the cock crowing. He has hard work getting rid of a feeling that this calm bodes no good.

Hilda is going away into service. She cries a little when she hears of it; for some reason it brings Mother into her mind. She raises no objections, however, but is soon wholly rapt up in her coming departure. She talks and spends more time with the other children than before, and teaches them once more all the children's games she knows. Juha overhears the children asking: " What's a villa like? What's a rector? " And in between

Hilda sheds tears for her mother, for it is only two days to Saturday.

A strange, pure atmosphere reigns in the Toivola cabin during the preparations for Hilda's departure. These preparations are made without haste, and the prevailing sensation is one of waiting. Until a morning dawns when the family, awakening from sleep, remember that today Hilda is going.

The sun shines that day. It shines on Hilda's new greased-leather boots and white pigtail ribbon. In her traveling garb she is a marvelously fragile being, parted long ago from the others. She is going far away, to that strange place, and with Mother already gone everyone feels that the parting is forever. And this knowledge wraps her round with a curious glow. The children are grave. They are shut up in the cabin while father is seeing Hilda off. There they go, past the cow-house. Two little heads press close to the window, but the staring eyes cannot follow the traveler and her escort very far; the last they see is Hilda's heel, like a separate little image that quickly becomes distorted in a bubble in the glass. The children remain for some time with their noses flattened against the pane. Then they drop down from the bench into the empty room, where the pensive spirit of Hilda still seems to dwell.

A great or at any rate a unique event has occurred. The postman has brought something for Johan Toivola, Crofter. A letter and some newspapers have arrived for him. They had lain a week on the kitchen window-sill at the farm before Juha, coming to the farm to work, got them from the hand of the kitchen-maid.

" Toivola has turned Socialist, I see," joked the master when he saw Juha's copies of the *People's News*. Juha was amazed at receiving newspapers addressed to him. The letter was most likely from Hilda — though even that seemed queer to Juha.

" You read it, Ida," he begged.

" I'll read it if you'll hand it over."

" Don't give it to her," put in the master. " Might be a love-letter."

" Go on, read it," urged Juha.

" It's from Kalle — see, there's his name, Karlo Toivola, at the bottom," Ida remarked.

" Ay, but read it, so that I can hear what he says before I go off to my work."

The letter began: " My dear Father, Sister, and Brother," and then came the usual conventional phrases about snow-white paper, a cold penholder, and a warm hand " that cannot reach yours to link, so has to do it in ink." The writer declared that he was in good health and hoped they were enjoying the same blessing. " I am now a cab-driver or cabby and doing well, I am earning more than you country bumpkins not being skinned by a bloodsucking farmer and I am sending you the *People's News* so that you can learn about the proletariat. . . ."

The writer further reported that Hilda was now in

1 9 8

Tampere, or not exactly in Tampere, but at a villa near by, and that the mistress was a more genteel woman than any in your parish and had often hired him to drive her home from town. He had seen Hilda and had once been given coffee in her kitchen. . . .

" And so Mother is dead, I heard about her from old man Pirjola at the cab-rank and that is the worker's fate always to die and Ville lad is dead too. . . ."

The whole household listened while the letter was read aloud, and when it came to an end the master re- marked:

" Sounds like that fellow was as clever with his pen as with his tongue."

The letter and the newspapers aroused mixed feel- ings in Juha's breast. He had almost forgotten Kalle's existence, and for some reason there was something un- real to him in this sign of life. It was as though Kalle had fallen on evil ways, and that gave rise to suspicions about what Hilda might be doing. On the face of it he had to admit that both children had prospered beyond all expectation and climbed to heights you would never have thought any child of his and Rina's could reach. A liveried town cabby was next door to a gentleman in Juha's eyes; no better thing could happen to a crofter's son than to be beyond the need of toiling for dear life in fields or forests, taking things easy on a cabby's box. Only Juha had his doubts about Kalle's capacity to fill such a post honorably; he would have been easier in

his mind if he had heard that Kalle was a farm-hand
sleeping in the corner of another man's kitchen; though
of course the whole letter might be a pack of lies. With
Hilda it was different; she deserved her present luck
a good deal better. For her it was right not to have to
mess about in cow-dung, but only dust the furniture in
rich people's rooms. She had been humble and gentle
in her ways since her childhood. Only there was now
the fear that Kalle might be leading her, too, astray.

Thus as Juha walked home in the moonlight his
mind was strangely empty. The dreamlike harmonious
mood of the past weeks had vanished; his thoughts did
not run on ahead this time to the children in the warmth
of the cabin, but wandered far afield in the tracks of
Kalle's cab. There was an everyday look again about the
world although the moon was shining; he almost felt
like wanting to quarrel with somebody for a change.
"What does he think he is, a lout like him, prancing
about, a cabby, while I have to slave here? This very
minute I'm so tired I can hardly move my feet, and
when I get home there'll be the cow to tend. It was all
through him we had all that trouble with poor dead
Ville; cost a lot it did, too. Has he ever sent us anything? . . . Cabby. . . ."

Old Juha realized that he had not looked ahead much
in his lifetime; he had been beaten by his own rascally
son. The picture of life as something sour and silly
threatened to take hold of him again; the peace of

2 0 0

these last weeks seemed to be taking its rightful place
beside the fancies that had led to his summer visit to
Tuorila and to be sharing their coloring. Again it was
as though he were returning crestfallen from a journey;
and now there wasn't even a wife waiting for him at
home. The moonlight made the cabin look like a dead
giant of olden times. If only Hilda were still at home.

Juha had no definite grounds for his bad humor, but
when, sitting beside the lamp, he began to glance through
the newspapers, the news in them made him more irritable than ever. He had a feeling of having been left
behind, in a freezing solitude. Yonder in the bed slept
two poor beings, brought into the world, but nothing
else. . . . And here he sat on this autumn night in the
heart of the woods, a man going on sixty.

Newspapers continued to come for him by every mail.
Juha read them in the evenings, his mood sullen and
quarrelsome. The articles he read did not especially interest him; they were written in the same cocksure aggravating style as Kalle's letter. They spoke of poverty
with a kind of pride, like badly brought up louts, or
with a sugary emotion that sickened Juha. They aroused
no enthusiasm in him. He read them as it were defi-
antly, to keep alive his own spite, now that life had again
toppled down to this level.

Daily existence with two helpless children was after
all a trial. He was too old to look after the cow properly;
he handled the milk clumsily. It had been stupid of

2 0 1

him to let Hilda go so far away. Yet it wouldn't be right
to tell her to come back; how was he to feed and clothe
her? And all at once Lempi's and Marti's case began to
look desparate to him too. " Suppose something happens
to me out here, what's going to become of them? And
what if I grow too old to work before they are able to
look after themselves? " Juha missed his wife. For all
her faults she had had her good points. While she was
in good health he had at least been able to sleep properly.
Now it was always as though he were being called upon
to sleep in a strange bed. Even while Hilda was at home
life had been easier.

Juha longed more and more for Hilda. Several times
he made up his mind in dull anger that he would have
her back. His present bad temper was harder to bear
than any irritability he had felt while his wife was alive.
His spite reached out farther this time, right to where
Kalle and Hilda were living, and a new element entered
into it: the threat of approaching helpless old age.

But then came an event that resolved his questionings
for a time — for the last time before everything was
resolved for him.

A day had come again when Juha had to be at the farm.
The times had greatly altered; work began now at six.
And the work this time was mere messing about, nothing to do but keep the threshing machine fed. At twelve
the master blew a blast on the steam-whistle and the men
went in to dinner. The farm-hands went to the kitchen,

but Juha and another man who had to feed themselves went to their food-bags in the living-room. As on many other days.

Juha had taken a few swigs at his milk-flask, when Ida came into the living-room with his newspapers and said: " There's a letter for you as well."

The letter had only just come, fresh from the postman's hands. Ida had to read it for him, and when she opened it a ten-mark note fluttered to the floor. What could that mean?

Again the same opening phrases and wishes for good health . . . " and I have to break the sad news to you that your dear daughter Hilda is dead; she drowned herself in the lake the night before last when it was moonlight and the mistress was away. The mistress's son was at home, but he was upstairs just going to bed and didn't know anything about it until in the morning when it was too late.

" And Hilda is being buried the day after tomorrow in case you want to come, the mistress is paying for it, but she said she was not giving any wages as Hilda was such a short time with her that it only covers the funeral and I am putting in this ten marks for you to buy yourself something with and there is a notice in Wednesday's *People's News* about Hilda's death, it cost two marks, and news about it inside the paper, death is trying you hard, but it is the proletarian's lot to die and you ought to join the battle with us seeing that you are a worker and cast off the yoke of capitalism."

Juha's mind stopped working, so that for a little while he knew nothing of what was going on around him. He failed to see the mistress come angrily into the room to fetch Ida, who was looking up the paragraph about Hilda's death, nor did he hear her snap: " What's keeping you from your work? — and I won't have such papers read in this house! " Juha would have had cause to take offense at that. But he hardly noticed the mistress.

So Hilda, too, was dead. Hadn't that been perfectly clear when she went? Hadn't it been clear ever since she was a child? And as pictures of Hilda as she used to be rose in Juha's mind, he saw her, in all of them, hurrying to meet her death. The idea became ineradicably implanted in Juha's mind that Hilda had died an accidental death.

In other respects the news left Juha coldly miserable. No melancholy sense of liberation awoke in him this time. After dinner he returned to work along with the other men. On them the news of Hilda Toivola's death made little impression; they reacted to it as to a piece of news duly noted; it is not the kind of subject on which one can start a conversation while at work. There are more masculine matters to be bandied, especially with the master present. Deep below the surface of their remarks loomed the class problem. The master had to listen to veiled barbs bearing on that problem. With the self-confidence of superior wisdom he talked his own common sense. At such moments the work instinctively quickened in pace. Old Toivola finally said something so downright ugly that the other men grinned. The master controlled himself with an obvious effort.

" Even an old ram soon gets swelled up with democracy, I see, particularly when he gets it in cab-loads."

The bow had never been drawn so taut before on this farm. The atmosphere was strained after that right up to supper-time. The work in hand seemed to withdraw into itself and become a separate entity, making three stiffly aloof elements in all: the master, the men and the job. The three together formed as it were a closed field of energy, so enormously much bigger, rawer, and more masculine than the death of any Hilda that to include them in one and the same thought was unnatural in a distasteful manner.

No feeling of liberation came to lighten this new blow. No sense of roots being torn out, no longing for compensation. Juha's mood was keyed to an evil pitch as he strode along his forest track that evening. The moon shone, but its right-hand rim had already shrunk and its light fell chill on the crazy cabin. No pensive light of past days shone from it; it was wholly of the present. It seemed to be hastening to complain to him that it was sorely in need of repairs, that it lay on land belonging to an enemy, was the property of that enemy, and that inside it were two human beings whose existence was not especially desirable.

The road onward was clear.

THE REBEL

 Iᴛ would be hard to think of a more purely artificial subject for study than the precise nature of Juha Toivola's attitude towards that time of national distress known as the period of Russian oppression. Juha Toivola's own sufferings during that period were no more remarkable than at any other time, nor could he observe in the small world in which he dwelt any other sufferings out of the ordinary. The master of the farm, at any rate, did not suffer, for he grew steadily richer; during those years his cattle increased from twelve cows in milk to eighteen, his horses by two. His manner towards his men had become more closed and at the same time more irritable — bossier, the men put it.

No, the master did not suffer, nor to any new extent did Juha. The uncertainty of his position began, to be sure, to be revealed to Juha about that time; he had no contract, and the best forests on the farm lay around his cabin. But in some ways things had improved. The working-day had shrunk from fifteen to twelve hours and the work was easier; the old threshing machine turned by hand had given way to one worked by a horse, and that again to a steam machine; scythes were now needed on the farm only to open the ends of plots. True, one of the new machines, the separator, changed the former full-bodied buttermilk into a thin blue liquid and led to the substitution of " vegetable " butter, known among the farm-hands as " blossom," for good honest butter.

People of Juha's type could not with the best will in the world have said what had all of a sudden made the situation of the Finnish " people " so exceedingly difficult. As the farmers were obviously growing fatter and there were no signs of impoverishment or leanness in the gentlemen living in the parishes, the lowly people were utterly at a loss to know what the distress and confusion in those quarters was about. " Their jobs must be in some kind of danger," they thought.

Schools were organized in private houses, and jolly enough those were. Big men could be seen sitting on benches and displaying considerable gifts for picking out the countries of Europe on the map, but there were also boys who joined the girls in giggling when the flaxen-haired young gentleman, with tears in his eyes, related the history of the " fatherland." The home schools dried up before long, but not before many brains had been shaken into life by the impulses gained from them, brains which thereafter began to think matters over on their own account.

Juha was not even among those influenced by the schools. He heard talk about them — there was one in his own village — but in his opinion they were tarred with the same brush as many other meetings and lectures; at bottom, however skillfully the fact might be hidden, they all aimed at one and the same thing: at prying money out of the people. Juha was convinced that even at the " home schools " some kind of ticket would have to be bought before all was over — it stood to reason, for how else were such schoolmasters to starch their collars? And he felt a mild satisfaction at knowing that he had never felt tempted to go, never been tricked. He might not have known how to get rich, but he had never been so childish as to go and pay for any tickets.

Such was Juha's relation to the period of oppression; even to speak of it somehow has an artificial ring. It was to him on a par with the Young People's Company or whatever its name was in the church village, which had its own tricks for parting soft young farm-hands and servant-girls from their money.

In the circumstances the first General Strike passed him by, its purpose entirely uncomprehended. Of course he knew about it — he had ears — but in all the talk there was something that irritated Juha. That there was some trickery at the bottom of it Juha was convinced, and a remark of Rinne's, who was spokesman for the workers, after the strike had been called off, stuck in his mind. Rinne said: " The workers polished the gentlemen's buttons."

Juha set no value on the vote to which he, too, had become entitled, and at the first elections he didn't trouble to vote. His private life gave him enough to think about, the year before the deaths in the family. " Let those vote who haven't my troubles. It won't give them bread."

It was after the General Strike of 1905 that the workers' movement really got under way in Finland; after eager agitators had begun to tour the country, associations sprang up and newspapers appeared to fan the blaze. Three years after the strike Juha Toivola declared himself a " temocrat," and in all probability he was one, but — incredible as it may sound — neither the strike, nor the agitators, and certainly not the newspapers had done anything to bring this about; they had no influence whatever over polka-clipped, bald Juha. He could not be bothered to go traipsing after agitators from his remote cabin. Newspapers came into his hands, and mostly he read them, or such parts as happened to strike his eye, news of frauds and offers of marriage, until after Hilda's death he stopped spelling his way through them; he had never put any faith in such tales.

The night after the letter telling of Hilda's death came, Juha lay outstretched on his bed, unable to sleep. He let his mind dwell first on Hilda's departure and on his own share in it — her death as such did not occupy his mind much. A faint moonlight filled the room; he could hear Lempi and Martin breathing. At moments

like this, when time and locality are only vaguely appre-
hended, even the weakest brain flits with the greatest
ease over wide territories of thought. A crofter in his
fifties who has lost a wife and children cannot help
thoughts of his own death coming into his mind and,
above all, of the slice of life still left to him. Hour after
hour passes; he takes the quid from his mouth and puts it
back again, gets up for a drink of water and lies down
again. He has a sensation of lying in a windy deserted
room; sleep refuses to enter there. The two children
sleeping like that in this silence are dreadfully alien to
him; they are children whose arrival in the world was
no signal for rejoicing, children left behind by their
mother.

So long as an old crofter has a wife, even a bad wife,
and growing children — in other words, a family and
household — his burden may be as heavy as it possibly
can be and yet his life will be a full one: a continuous
tenacious living, level, hard, and free from thought. In
a sense he has laid down his burden and makes no attempt to carry it farther.

And so it goes on for years. Until the sleepless night
comes when he discovers that not even this burden is
left to him. Death has been liberal with its mercies.
But now ease becomes a burden. Around him is emptiness, a drear emptiness left after his deliverance from
his burden, a vacuum attracting thoughts over which he
has no control; and for an untrained mind that is misery.
With the great encompassing atmosphere of a household

lost to him, he sees with pitiless clarity the countless minor deficiencies of his life. He has seen them of course before this, on occasions when he was alone and away from the household, but above them was that which awaited him at home: his wife, children, cow — in a word, the household. However wretched it was, it was something to which each member of the family unconsciously clung for protection; while it existed, even God was as though a feature of it. Now this solid center of things has dropped out; the flat expanse of all-life has risen to a level with the ego. The two sleeping children have become encumbrances, minor matters the main thing.

Deep under the surface of Juha's waking mood an instinctive desire for new company was already stirring. This deserted cabin was not home — why, even Hilda would never be coming back to it. . . .

And so, about this time, a new trait could be observed in Juha Toivola; he began to hang about the village and drop in at houses where he was known, to sit and jaw for hours at a stretch. He criticized the way of the world, his voice rising and becoming almost angry. His observations were colored throughout by a tacit intimation that he had examined it all in person and that these were his conclusions, not those of an ordinary common "temocrat." In his talk phrases like "as the Saviour says" still tended to crop up.

"Old Toivola was prophesying again half the day at

our place," the village women would remark to one another.

After carrying on thus for hours, Juha would return home gloomier than ever. As he walked through the forest he would feel as though he had been straightening matters out for a pack of strangers or as though he had undertaken a long, complicated business on their behalf. The feeling was distasteful to him, for in his fundamental character there was no love for his fellow-men. He had endured them, having had to put up with them since his childhood. But never had human beings — in the mass, as they fill this world — been wholly well disposed towards him, neither poor nor rich.

Thus in reality philanthropic ideals were alien to Juha's nature. But life is made up of conflicting forces, and some obstinate force arising out of accidental events in his career drove him to hold forth on this ideal of " temocracy " in other people's houses. This force is, as it were, related to the circumstance that the cabin is cold to him and refuses to warm him. He has got to preach to other people. And in these abstract discussions he is never wholly in agreement with anyone else. However clearly he may grasp the truth of some " temocratic " principle or other enunciated by another man, he will not nod his head in agreement, but has to invent his own often very obscure grounds for it which the other speaker had failed to observe, true as his grasp of the principle may have been. Old Toivola simply has to prophesy.

And he goes on prophesying, marking time, as it

were, without getting any farther, for many years, while the Finnish labor movement, under the guidance of its young starched-collared leaders, grows and develops. Those white-collar men are alien, almost abhorrent to him, for he cannot get rid of his old suspicion that, to some extent at least, they are out to line their own pockets. A white-collar man, again, hearing Juha spouting, would regard him with lack-luster, embarrassed eyes.

And so it went on until the World War came, bringing with it the sufferings by which mankind was to be purified for the historical duties set the twentieth century. Only the people, because their souls were an inheritance from the nineteenth century, sat reading their newspapers in the late summer evenings, trying to guess which side would win and meanwhile going on living in the belief that afterwards everything would be as before; it was pleasantly exciting to be living in such stirring times. The war would be over by Christmas, people thought, but when a second Christmas came and there was still no sign of its coming to a close, they began to feel anxious, unconsciously divining that the matter would not end with a victory achieved by force of arms, but would be followed by even longer complications.

In the circumstances the clash of arms became a period of respite, and incredibly it proved that while the terrible carnage was going on, people were less disciplined in their lives than in times of peace; they lived during the deluge as mankind was formerly said to live before a

deluge. The principles and ideals which the previous
century had tinkered with in the intervals between business were revealed as ink and paper only. One of the
pitiful sights of the age was to see men of ripe age sitting
beside their deflated ideals, pitiful because they seemed
really to have believed in them. Youth was happier,
having for long refused to believe in those ideals. Youth
roamed the streets and highways, danced and made
merry, and some mysteriously vanished in circumstances strongly tinged with a flavor of forbidden high
politics. (Actually they had gone to Germany, to learn
soldiering with a view to a coming separation from
Russia.) On the whole, life was a day-to-day affair.

Until the crash came in Russia. In all secrecy that
crash left an unpleasant taste of disappointment
in many Finnish mouths. What was to come next,
now that good business and abundant employment on
fortification works were suddenly at an end? Having
recovered its balance a little, the nation hastened to
manifest its admirable faithfulness to the indivisibility
of the Empire. In token of this faithfulness various
kisses and signatures were exchanged, all without criti-
cism of any kind at the time, though the press was then
free. The affair of the vanished youths, their destination now an open secret, was deplored; by the laws of
Finland they were guilty of high treason in seeking out
the enemy for military training for a rising that the
Russian Revolution had now made unnecessary. This
phase of faithfulness endured up to the Bolshevik Revo-

lution, which from being a crime gradually became a political *fait accompli*. By then the independence movement was being openly discussed in ordinary citizen circles.

In his own submerged depths Juha Toivola continued to exist as before; indeed, at this moment he was as actively engaged in creating history for his nation as anyone.

On a beautiful May morning, when the scent of the earth and its vegetation was at its sweetest and touches of yellow already caught the eye along the banks of ditches, Juha might have been seen approaching the village, warmed by his walk, his eyes in his hairy face glittering wide-awake and restless. He looks younger than ten years ago; with summer coming on like this — and for other reasons as well — there seems to be less cause for worry. He enjoys the knowledge that he is going to spend the day in the open lands. He is not going to the farm to work, but to Rinne's place.

Earlier that spring Juha had happened to be in the church village the day the funeral of the victims of the Revolution was being celebrated. People streamed in from all directions in long columns; red flags fluttered even in the ranks of some of the columns. Juha reached the Kuuskoski cross-roads just as the column of workers from the paper-mill came along. A voice from the ranks with a touch of brusqueness ordered Juha to fall in. Juha retorted: "I know my place as well as you do," and fell into line.

Marching there, he stared at the red neck of the young man who had ordered him about, thinking: " Who do you fancy you are? " The columns met at the Young People's Society building and a meeting was soon under way. Some of the gentlemen in the village had hoisted blue and white flags, and the meeting fell to discussing what action was to be taken in regard to this counter-revolutionary demonstration.

Still irritated by the brusqueness with which he had been ordered to join the marchers, Juha spoke at the meeting, for the first time in his life. He was stared at, and Juha enjoyed that. His speech was brief and wholly irrelevant to the matter at issue, yet it had the result that he was elected to the deputation that went to demand the removal of the offending colors. The leader of the deputation was the same red-necked Kuuskoski man who had officiously taken upon himself to give orders to Juha, but Juha, as the oldest "temocrat" present, had his say as well. And his words were far from polite. When, later in the day, the gentry discussed the day's happenings, they asked one another, " Who was that tangle-faced old fellow? He was about the worst of the lot."

So Juha became drawn into the swelling turmoil of the times, and he remained faithful to the call almost to the end. On his return that day to his home his thoughts still ran high with defiance even in the solitude of his forest track. He seemed still to see before him all the new faces that had stared at him during the day, first at the meeting, then in the homes of the gentry. All those faces inspired in him the same faintly spiteful feeling. He needed no one to order him about; he knew what he was doing . . . "They don't know the first thing about temocracy — telling me. . . ."

The cabin came into sight, as on a thousand other evenings. "Evict me from this home, would they?" thought Juha, and for the first time for long, plans for the future began to form in his mind. Winter was over too. . . .

The next time Juha worked on the farm he had so much to say while he worked that the master uttered a curse.

"Hold your tongue!" he snapped; "I'm the man who says what there is to say here."

"We'll see about that," Juha retorted in a lower voice.

And now it was to be seen, for on this May morning Juha is not going to work, but to Rinne's place. The strike epidemic has spread to this parish. The dairy has been permitted to go on working so far, but now a stop is going to be put to that as well. The day will show whether any of the farmers are thinking of showing fight.

Juha walks as though he was on the way to church, feeling at his best both inside and out. A masculine feeling of security fills his bosom. When he reaches the open village lands and calls to mind the owners of the various fields, he cannot help smiling. He was here yesterday with a lot of other men staring out the scabs, and today the fields wear a different aspect. Formerly the sight of growing crops aroused in his mind pictures of the master and his locked granaries; now it only reminds him of what the workers have planned to do today. The wealth of the open lands is like the common wealth of mankind.

Juha's own master was out on the lake trying his nets when he saw Juha emerge from the forest track. The distance between them was big enough to allow the master freely to stare after that old fellow, whom he knows too well for his own liking. The fellow is so old, so poor, and so settled in his ignorance and brainlessness that the hate the master cannot help feeling for him is unpalatable even as he admits its existence. He cannot help hating, yet at the same time he senses something touchingly hopeless in the seriousness of the man. The present unrest, the murmur of which seems to pulse in the air, is another matter; grave enough to awaken anxiety, yet fraught with something before which the deepest, loneliest soul of a man is helpless and secretly inclined to submission. At odd moments the master has felt the desire to surrender to the mighty subterranean current, but when his eye falls on the tangled beard and stupid, pricking eyes of a disgusting old fellow like Juha, his stomach turns and he knows hate, the hate that springs from a conflict of one's own making.

Everywhere similar private little decisions are well-ing up in people's minds and uniting to form the tense pressure of those revolutionary days. That pressure comes to a head and finds vent in incidents like that which is now taking place in the dairy yard. Cries fill the air there and are succeeded by a defiant speech; in the bigger crowd one sees tightened chins and glances; in the smaller opposing group, furious looks. The crowd remains in the yard until noon and then scatters; the show is over for the day in this neighborhood. In the evening the events of the day are debated in many dwellings. No one bothers any longer to argue about right or wrong; men are content to describe to one another with a curious feverish liveliness the actions and methods of the other side. When night falls the farmers carefully lock their doors and settle down to sleep in their board-lined and painted houses. Over their long files of rooms still hovers the old assurance of peace in the home.

But on the highway and in the village lanes shadowy figures are in movement. Cigarettes glow and sometimes a roar of laughter breaks out. Three farm-maids come strolling along the road, all three with white kerchiefs on their heads that glow softly in the night. A party of men join them, and they all go together into a tiny shack where lemonade and cakes used to be sold. There are over a dozen of them, and no patriot could ever divine what thoughts pass between them.

So much for that gang. Juha Toivola knows nothing of their doings. He has fussed around all day, and in the evening dragged himself wearily into his woods. In his mind there is now no room for doubts or hair-splitting; these last few days he has given up " prophesy-ing." He sees only the farmers and the resistance put up by them. That makes the situation clear and whole; it is all in harmony with the billowing spirit of the times. Old Juha was filled with the revolutionary fever that summer.

And the Revolution goes on, swelling with a sense of its own importance. Every morning the mail brings newspapers which tell of the growth of the movement throughout the country, from Helsinki upward. The fairest summer of the Finnish proletariat is dawning. Weeks come when not a flutter is to be seen anywhere of the capitalist newspapers which always lie and distort the facts in their attempts to combat the truth of the workers' movement. On the harvest-field nobody takes any notice when the master tries to set an example and in a fury erects the shocks on three whole plots unaided. It is almost a pleasure to watch his helpless rage while the men sit around for hours whetting and testing their sickles. The former competitions between man and man to see who reached the end of a plot first are for-gotten. The summer of the proletariat in Finland — 1917. Free, head proudly erect, the young laborer saun-tered along the summery lanes; the crofter felt a new affection for his fields, from which breathed an inspir-ing promise. . . .

Yet in every phase of every stratum of the Finnish

people everything turns mostly to tragedy, a strange thin tragedy. Fate, instead of exterminating the nation, has subjected it to slow torture. It lets the sun emerge, but no sooner are we so intoxicated with our good fortune that we are at a loss whom to embrace than it hastens to reveal that it was only playing with us.

Winter had come; January. Snowstorms, frosts, bright starlit nights when time seems to have stopped and to be listening in the silent forests back through the decades, and the thud of snow falling from a branch is like a deep unintentional sigh in an hour of devotion. In this form winter has returned again and again for generations, and along the narrow winter tracks people have moved whose deepest instinct has been attuned to that devout stillness.

So it has been; not now.

Few have time even to notice that winter has come; why, only yesterday it was November, when the Butcher Guards were scattered. The taxpayers' strike is only three weeks old — and now the slogan is: "Not a stiver to the Church either." An old crofter cannot sit quiet at home in times like these. At home, in the lonely cabin, the sluggish stillness of former times seems to lie in wait on gray days, and who could revert to that now? Instinctively one flees from silence. "What is going to happen in Parliament? Are the capitalists going to legalize the Butcher Guards? Then it is time we lads rose as well. What, after all, is Parliament? We lost the

elections — well, what then? — we lost, by God; what
about it? Parliament is an old woman's game; the bourgeoisie always hampering us there, lose or win. No
matter how large a majority the workers might have
there, it makes no difference so long as there are capitalists and the storehouse keys hang on their walls.
Parliament and majorities mean nothing to us. We'll
give them majority. If it comes to a pinch, there's more
of us."

As when a proper fellow at a name-day dance begins
to feel his gorge rise at the sight of coffee-tables and
other sickening finickinesses — he gives a yell and hits
out.

Juha Toivola no longer has as many household cares
as before; Lempi is fourteen and able to look after the
cow, especially now that it is not giving milk. Ten years
have thus gone by since that death-summer when Juha
paid his visit to his relatives at Tuorila. It was one of
those old-fashioned summers of endless sizzling heat.
Juha no longer thinks about his dead and his relatives;
they have nothing to do with the present. The crofter
problem is now to the fore; that and the Butcher
Guards.

Juha sits in houses where he is known and preaches
in a squeaky voice. In the evenings he goes home,
yawns, and thinks of hardly anything at all. The room
with its beds and rags has acquired a new aspect with
the passage of time. Poverty formerly dwelt here, but
poverty has now given way to a vague but real destitu-

tion; the old atmosphere of a home has evaporated from
the elements that compose it, and the room now calls
to mind the living-room of a big farm after a bunch
of tramps temporarily taken on to work have gone, leaving behind them a coarse humorless lewdness vibrating
in the air.

One might believe this new aspect of misery to be an
illusion only, were it not for the fact that visible wit-
nesses testify to its reality — lice. There are now lice
in the Toivola beds. And pensive night-thoughts for-
sake the bed where there are lice. The louse is not an
unconscientious or an accidental visitor; nor is its well-
being contingent on dirt. It may keep away from the
most dilapidated shack, but it invariably spreads slowly
and surely where humanity, in the abstract sense of the
word, trembles on the verge of extinction, as in front-
line trenches, labor barracks, and other places where
workers are deposited.

At Toivola both want and misery now reign. When
autumn came Juha was refused admittance to the farm-
households, members of which are entitled to the special
rations allowed to grain-growers. He has to fetch the
small ration which his bread-card entitles him to buy
from the church village. Thus for days at a time the
family goes hungry, with potatoes and the brine-water
from pickled sprats as sole diet. Lempi and Martin
mostly feast on these by themselves, for Juha is nearly
always away; often even nights. Those two thin-necked
hollow-eyed beings have managed to survive. Gray and

slow of movement they crouch under their comfortless rags, two images of misery personified. They attend no school, not even the school of life.

Juha likes best to be in the village, away from home. He is continually whispering in the ear of now this " comrade," now that — he is forced to beg for small loans. Rinne — who knows what that man is? An impenetrable fellow, a sly and cunning agitator — does old Toivola a good turn now and then on the quiet. He lets Juha do little jobs for the union, jobs Juha can be trusted to carry out, and presses a few marks into his hand in reward. Rinne is much in demand, still working together with the bourgeoisie on the many boards of which he is a member. His brows are always puckered in a frown; he opens his mouth only to give curt explanations. He merely smiles when Juha starts preaching on any subject. Nevertheless, Rinne is a better man than any farmer.

But when a man's affairs are in a bad state, they often get worse and are finally at their worst. One Wednesday the situation at Toivola was such that there had been no bread in the house for the last twenty-four hours, not a wisp of hay was left for the cow, and Juha could think of no way out of his difficulties. The cow would be calving in five weeks' time, and it was a pity to feed her only on alder-shoots. Yet it was not easy to go and beg from Rinne again so soon. And where was Rinne to find hay for the cow? The children dipped their potatoes in brine-water and swallowed in heavy gulps. At last Juha made up his mind to go to the village; he would drop in at Rinne's, but say nothing about his plight. The children began sobbing softly, guessing that Father would be away all night, going off at this late hour.

Old Toivola drew near to Rinne's house with a sensation of being about to call on his betters — the past few weeks had brought out in Juha the trait of character that once sent him to Tuorila. But when he set foot in Rinne's living-room he realized at once that his visit was ill-timed. Rinne was too busy to bother with him. Rinne's voice could be heard from the parlor; there were several other men there, and by the sound of their voices one could guess that they had not assembled to talk about the weather, and not assembled casually. Rinne's wife took in a tray with coffee, and Rinne popped out to see who the newcomer was. He gave a well-simulated friendly answer to Juha's greeting and went back into the parlor.

When Rinne's wife came out, she said to Juha: " Now then, Toivola, why don't you go into the parlor? A lot of the others are there."

" Do you think I might? "

" Why not? — I suppose Toivola can come in, can't he? " she shouted through the door. The answer was unintelligible, but she said: " Go on in."

Juha went into the parlor and sat down beside the door. He had the same feeling as when a farmer had happened to invite him into the house. Here too were cigarettes and coffee-cups, tablecloths on the tables, and pictures on the walls. Juha had no idea why all the workers' leaders were assembled in such style on a week-day, in their best clothes and high-shafted top-boots. Must be a special kind of meeting.

Juha ought not really to have been sitting there like that. It would have been a different matter if there had been bread and hay at home. He tried uneasily to put in a word now and again, though he had no clear idea what the discussion was about. Something about the ridge at Kuuskoski, what it is like at various points along its length. Juha knows the ridge as well as anybody.

" It's an easy place to defend," he remarked. " Shall we be needing it for that sort of thing? "

" Who knows how soon we shall be needing it? " one of the men answered.

And gradually, by venturing a question on every suitable occasion, Juha found out what had happened. War had broken out. War — no one utters the word; it is like an all too overwhelming sum total of certain preceding factors. War — is it a real war if the Red Guards and the Butchers clash? Will it not rather be something like what happened in the dairy yard in the summer, a demonstration? No one can do anything to a demonstration, the demonstrators are so many. It seems too fantastic to think that anyone could start firing on such a crowd.

More men arrived in the living-room, and Rinne went out to meet them. While he was away Juha tried to find out what the others thought of the turn events had taken, speaking in a whisper as though he had been afraid to speak while Rinne was in the room. Juha's affairs are in a bad state at home; how is this going to affect them?

Six men arrived in the living-room; Juha caught a glimpse of shotguns. Up to now the meeting in the parlor had been the center of things; it now broke up. There was a general move to the living-room, where among those present are a few of the village roughs. Some of them have been in prison, and hitherto Juha has instinctively regarded them as men unfit for any serious purposes. But now there is an uplifted spirit in the air that makes any such distinctions invidious. The cigarette-smoke grows thicker. The moment is all that matters now; there is no yesterday and no tomorrow. Every time even a couple of men arrive, the mass-spirit seems to double in strength. Sentry duties are already being planned for the night. Quite as a matter of course, uninvited, Juha spends the night in the house. The afternoon, when he left his cabin because there was neither bread nor hay, is far distant. The other men have all had similar matters to think about only a little while ago. But not now.

The " Red reign " in the locality has begun. In the morning men already form up in ranks in Rinne's yard before going off in different directions to confiscate arms. By the evening the first requisition order has been served on a farmer; he brings a load of hay — to the barracks; the word has suddenly come into use. Men return from their search for arms; in such numbers that no one can remember when all of them came. A buzz of talk fills the smoke-enwrapped room; the men describe to one another what happened at each of the farms visited. Among the men are toughs whom Juha has never set eyes on before. Rinne is in the parlor with the same men as yesterday; they are the Staff. The barracks and the Staff — around these stretches the rest of the village, looking curiously estranged. Over yonder is Toikka's farm, yonder Paitula. What has happened in the church village?

Juha has one private little nightmare to incommode him; it is more than twenty-four hours since he left home. The surrounding din makes him unusually perceptive. He grasps that he had better not go home yet this evening either. As he eats his buttered bread and soup he tries to solve the problem: will the children and the cow be able to hold out another day? This evening and the coming night?

However rapidly an avalanche may grow, it needs its own time. And for success in that for which Juha is now waiting the avalanche will have to swell to considerable proportions. The third day was almost at an end before Juha's hopes were realized.

On that day one heard everywhere, hummed, whistled, bawled, piped by children, and screeched by women, from the rows of sleighs passing along the road, from lanes and farmyards:

Against the yoke of tyranny
From the earth an army rises.

And on that day one knew what it was to rule and tasted the sensation of liberty. The sensation of being free ran in cold shudders up and down old Juha's spine; his thin voice quavered as he tried to sing, when after agonized waiting his own private liberation came; when a load of hay went skimming along the forest track to Toivola, and Juha himself bore a heavy load of food from Rinne's to the children, who were half-dead with hunger and weeping. At last Juha could devote himself wholly to the cause of a greater, ideal liberty.

By that time matters had already reached a settled stage. The following night Juha met his son Kalle, a stout red-faced town cabby, now in command of a company. No father-and-son relation showed itself in their encounter; a condition for that was lacking: a gruff paternal authority on Juha's part. Kalle spoke to him as to any other man. The next morning he set off with his men in the direction of Kuuskoski.

Rumors were already current: such-and-such a great gentleman was no longer among the living. But such matters were not much discussed. One discussed the affairs of the local farmers and, to pass the time, subjected the character of each of them to a searching analysis. Tomorrow it would be a full week since this started. Life in the neighborhood had been violently dislocated during those first few days, but the dislocation soon became the normal state of things. The new situation had no particular name among the local people; it was what it was. One was shy about mentioning many of its details. Not until the Whites arrived did many learn that this was rebellion and the Finnish War of Independence.

The war has already lasted seven weeks. In many lukewarm hearts the high excitement of its early days has had time to fade; requisitionings of horses and food, permits to move about, all that had become customary and people were only mildly alarmed when a sleigh drove up to the house and they saw the familiar rifle-barrels with their cleaning-rods and red rosettes. Such callers were received with friendly smiles and promises to fulfill the orders they brought; old acquaintances from one's own parish — why not? And there goes the sleigh again down the yard. Soon the men from the front will be here for the milk.

Life is almost monotonous. In the twilight one visits neighbors, sits in living-rooms, and chats about what one had seen while driving here and there by command of the Reds or one repeats what Reds from other localities have said. One speaks of everything with a smile on one's lips and tries to keep on good terms with everybody.

One doubts whether the Butchers — no one uses any other term for the other side — will ever advance so far as this. Here a farmer has been given cigarettes while acting as coachman; he is now able to treat others to a smoke. Someone remarks that the master of Paitula is under orders to report to Rinne four times a day; nobody's business, that. Someone outside of it all even thinks to himself that a taste of humble pie will do the man good. A man says he has heard that Rinne's son has been killed; the same outsider feels almost grateful that the young hooligan is gone for good. The outsider believes he can see all the different chains of events that have led to the present situation. The times are a source of secret satisfaction to him, for nothing is happening except what had to happen; the only thing that troubles him is a mild impatience. Get through with it quicker! He knows that neither side is capable of victory. The first condition for that is victory over one's own self.

So run the thoughts of one secretly outside of it all and careful not to disclose himself; and now he feels in his nerves that events are moving. Life abhors a long monotony. Life is in general inclined to be passionate.

In the general hubbub Juha Toivola has continued to fuss about where anything is doing. The whole of this time he has been seen around here with his red ribbons and staring eyes. Many a farmer who had previously not even paid Juha the compliment of classing him with those Socialists has had to take orders from Juha. Juha likes to be present on every important occasion, his eyes starting out of his head, his mouth grimly pursed. He also likes to be sent to commandeer necessities, although his own master once sent word to the staff asking whether they hadn't a better man to send than Toivola. Many a man would rather give up half his land than be under orders from the likes of Juha. For some mysterious reason Juha is especially obnoxious to the farmers and the object of their hate. Juha, on his part, does not feel any great hate for the farmers. All he wants is that they should admit what he has always said: that the People are almighty and that living on another man's sweat will have to stop. They wouldn't listen to him before, and when he went into their kitchens would often not even so much as ask him to sit down. However politely he addressed them, they grunted and turned their attention elsewhere. Even now, with the war on, Juha has noticed that they have been boiling over with rage inside when he brought them their orders.

That is what it has all been like for Juha. Today more than one secret listener on the telephone has begun to suspect what may be happening shortly, but Juha — he still drives about the parish with Kalle Nieminen commandeering rugs. Juha's shrunken brains have felt no need to keep informed about the situation. He has so far been able to save well over five hundred marks. Not so bad, though nothing like what he thought he would get when things were put right. For although he knows that he will now get the cabin and fields for his own, and a bit of forest as well, he needs a good deal more money. He is even beginning to be a bit impatient. He has worked hard doing his bit and means to go on working, but results are slow in coming. Rinne, too, is maybe looking out for himself, with all that money passing through his hands.

He hints something of the sort to Kalle Nieminen, who sits beside him in the sleigh. But Kalle listens with one ear only, answers in a bored tone, hums, and stares ahead. Never, never in the whole of his life has Juha been able to find a real comrade. . . .

Dusk has fallen when Juha arrives with the plunder at Staff headquarters. He marches into the house, his hairy face in a solemn, preoccupied frown; he is an old man, but here he is, about and active — a rare state things would be in if everybody were to take it easy in the house. A man has to be up and doing when the times call for action. It is only as it should be when Rinne's wife invites him into the kitchen for a drop of coffee.

When Juha laps his coffee and lets a sense of luxury steal over him as at present, his mood is usually the same as in former days after he had been paid for some job or other, and the money, all the while he was sipping his coffee, agreeably exercised his thoughts. The fascination of a steady settled activity tickles and worries him in equal parts. He feels secure in his surroundings; men always around him, warmth, food, coffee, movement. Someone always going off somewhere, the telephone busy, and everything gliding along smoothly.

Has anyone thought of bringing wood into the kitchen? No, the pile seems to be running low — I'll have to fetch some.

The rumble that has been sounding for weeks from the front at Kuuskoski is also a familiar and snug noise by now; it belongs to the situation; without it life wouldn't be what it is. The long files of hundreds of sleighs down on the ice seem to move of their own accord, needing no boss to tell them where to go; sometimes word comes that so-and-so from these parts has fallen, and, curiously, the news only adds to the sense of security. Juha does not even want to be a farmer; he is comfortable like this. Juha, as it were, cloaks himself in the bustle of the continuous activity; nothing could be more unnatural than that his brains should seek to work out the significance and consequences of the situation. He feels all right as he is, and in any case he imagines himself to be safely hidden in the crowd, come what may. For what does he signify among all these thousands, that anybody should specially single him out? He goes to fetch wood for the kitchen.

Juha is a hustler and the members of the Staff invariably eye him and speak to him with an approving smile. Juha is aware of this and accepts their approval with a show of gruffness. This very minute, only just back from a round of the parish, he is fetching wood. In the living-room other men sprawl on the beds; one man sits in the rocking-chair reading a newspaper.

Yet this evening Juha cannot help stealing inquisitive

glances at the members of the Staff; for some reason he is haunted by a dreadful suspicion that their calmness is assumed. It began already when he returned from commandeering those rugs. The telephone, taken from one of the farms, seemed to look down from the wall with a wooden expression; from the ceiling hung the electric lamp installed there " by order." Nobody took the slightest notice of his helpfulness. Indeed, one might almost have thought that they had had enough of his eternal fussing. As he went out, the thought flashed into Juha's mind that this new life had now lasted seven weeks.

And nothing has really changed. The evening is calm; even the firing at Kuuskoski has quieted down a little. Still hanging on there, the Butchers. . . . A sentinel stands at the gate. From the road comes the sound of footsteps; two people are approaching. One is a man, the other a woman; both wear good fur coats and both are silent. There they go, gentlefolk, the master of Paitula reporting at headquarters, accompanied as usual by his wife. The firing at Kuuskoski becomes more and more desultory. Is anything special happening? There is such a funny feeling in the air.

Juha goes into the shed and dispiritedly gathers an armful of wood. What is all this? He stops in the middle of a movement and stares into the darkness: " This is Revolution and I am a revolutionary." It had been pleasant to mutter that to oneself when it all began, but now it seems to hold meanings too deep for Juha to penetrate. " If we could all go back to the old order now; I have saved well over five hundred marks, and that's something to the good." A dreadful feeling that there is no more going back for him overwhelms Juha. The master of Paitula has vanished into the house, and the silence around Juha is unbroken.

When Juha returns to the house with his load the master of Paitula is standing in the living-room near the door; he stands in his usual haughty gentleman's attitude; his face is dark red, his jaw is thrust out. Rinne is questioning him again. As Juha passes with his load behind the gentleman's back he hears him answer Rinne in a violent tone and with a self-conscious jerk of his body. Juha takes the wood into the kitchen, comes back into the living-room, and in reply to the gentleman's recent remark says:

" Capital's been oppressing the poor people's liberty so long that it's neither here nor there if one gent has to use his legs a little."

Juha's words break in on the genuine suspense of the moment with the effect of a tactless interruption by a poor relative. Rinne is seated on one of the beds with his elbows on his knees, a cigarette between his fingers; he gives a grimace as though to say to the gentleman: " You think we depend on the likes of Juha, but if you do, you're mistaken." Aloud he says to the master of Paitula with an impatient movement:

" Well, there's no need for you to come any more, if you think it healthier not to. You can go."

" Good," answered the gentleman, and turning, he left the room. Rinne too got up from the bed and went out. The men left in the living-room were silent, each in the attitude he had assumed awhile ago. Only Juha tried to say something, but nobody heeded him. The telephone rang. Lahteenmaki got up to answer.

" Hello — yes — no, it's not him — I couldn't say, he went out a couple of minutes ago — what's that? — Haven't the Turku men? — What? gone! Where? — That's the Devil's own lie — "

Lahteenmaki hung up the receiver, but made no remark.

" I feared as much," said Mäkinen.

Juha was vaguely uneasy, though he hadn't understood what the call was about. Rinne came in.

" You go, Toivola, and keep an eye on that Butcher. See he doesn't leave his lair."

" What Butcher? "

" The one that just left here. Any telephone message? " Rinne asked, turning to the others.

" Yes."

" Shall I take my rifle? " asked Juha.

" Of course," answered Rinne with a curiously loud laugh.

Juha Toivola is leaving Rinne's house for the last time, though he does not know it yet. The span of sixty years that began on a night round about Michaelmas so far back in the past that it is hard to imagine any living link between that night and these warlike times is drawing to a close. In that past, splint torches flickered and old Benjamin Nikila in his burlap smock spent his days drunk with home-made spirits, beat his third wife, and ruled over his household, and between heaven and earth reigned a deep country peace. The boy born in those times — all the other members of the household have gone to their eternal rest — has become the Socialist who walks yonder along the road. His brains are of the simplest, the horizon of his mind the narrowest conceivable, and yet he has survived through the sixty years which we know to have been the most eventful, the richest in development, in the history of his people.

As he stalks there along the dark wintry road, with his beard, his staring eyes and his rifle, one can almost see perched on his lean shoulders the Puckish spirit of human progress; tongue in cheek, jerking and hopping, it urges old Juha Toivola onward. And seen in this fashion Juha is by no means a repulsive individual, rather does he arouse in the beholder a half-humorous sympathy. For how often has not the same imp grinned gleefully from the shoulders of many who tread their path with broad brows furrowed with deep lines of wisdom?

A sense of lonely helplessness is uppermost in Juha's mind as he strides on towards Paitula. Important events are brewing on this eve of St. Mary's Day, though Juha has no clear inkling of the direction they are to take. All he suspects is that he has been sent on an errand no one else would be bothered with, and he feels that he is being badly rewarded for all his wood-carrying and helpfulness.

That, however, has been his fate all his life long; it is something neither Juha nor anyone else can help. To be spurned by others and to find out that whatever efforts he has made, he has always, as it were, chosen the wrong moment; that is Juha's fate. Other men rise and fall in the world in a natural manner; even their misfortunes are of a kind to be taken seriously. Whereas with Juha, in all his good and bad luck alike, there is always the same leaven of poor taste.

This present money-getting, too, and his rising prosperity in general — it still remains to be seen whether any good will come of it. . . . When his wife died a wave of harmony had welled up inside him. He felt then that he was being kind to the children and was confident that his life would thereafter proceed smoothly from that new start. He planned in his mind how this and that was bound to be easy now that the mother had left them. And things did really seem to be shaping well; an especially promising omen was the luck his girl had in finding employment with real full-blooded gentlefolk. Juha felt such an access of strength at that time that it was not at all hard for him to go about with a ten-mark note in his pocket for a week without wanting to spend it.

What Juha specially remembers about those days is, curiously enough, that the moon shone with unusual brightness. . . . It was the brightest time of Juha's life as well. But then when the girl died like that, everything crashed to its former level, and Juha awoke to the old familiar life, full from morning to eve with one thing and another, but never satisfying. Juha had to find something to occupy himself with, something which, although it was only a kind of stuffing and with a touch of absurdity at that, like dressing up in a white collar, had to be if he was to escape being looked down on as a simpleton. As stuffing there appeared this " temocrat " business, which was then being preached in so many living-rooms, as before that " this matter of salvation " had been preached.

Juha had crossed the ice and reached the Paitula yard-gate. The house was silent and dark. Across the channel the lights of Rinne's headquarters twinkled, and farther away two big carbon lamps cast a glow over the church village. From the same direction came a steady thin crackle from Kuuskoski; a single sleigh was climbing the slope towards Paitula. It drew nearer and Juha distinguished rifle-barrels and two turned-up fur collars.

" Who goes there? " Juha asked gruffly.

No answer came from the depths of the fur collars, and the horse broke into a trot.

A whole hour then passed during which Juha saw nobody; the stars only winked mysteriously and the fitful crackle from afar was like the stern voice of this solemn night. Juha could look about him in peace and try to picture the life led by the gentleman, that incomprehensible being. The brains, riches, and habits of the master of Paitula — Juha seemed to see them before him and was nearly angry at the contradiction he seemed to see in them. He tried to remember the occasions on which he had come into contact with the fellow.

The proletariat and the master of Paitula — how helpless a gentleman like him is in the face of the people! On the one hand the master's brains and schemes, for he, too, wanted to get on in the world — on the other the brains of the proletariat. The gentleman's brains skulk in the parlor yonder, whereas the proletariat's brains surge as it were from one end of the world to the other.

Sleighs were coming his way again. There must be a long row of them, to judge from the sound. What sleighs could they be, coming in such numbers from that direction?

When the leading sleighs were abreast of Juha, a voice demanded roughly:

" Hey you, old fellow, have two men driven past here? "

" Two went past here an hour ago."

" Hell's traitors — why didn't you stop them? "

Three or four sleighs passed, and again Juha was hailed.

2 4 4

" Hey, old man, did two officers come this way? "

" Yes, I saw them."

" How long ago was that? "

" About an hour."

Hard-driven horses continued to pass. In the sleighs five or six, sometimes as many as eight men were crowded. Women sat in the men's laps.

From one sleigh came a shout: " Clear out, old man, the front's busted! "

But the exhortation had no effect on Juha — he was in the grip of a stronger mass-suggestion. Similar cries and questions continued to be hurled at him.

" Got a Butcher rounded up there, or what are you squatting there for? "

Juha ought to have been aware by now that the files of sleighs spelled retreat; perhaps in his subconscious mind he understood. But uppermost was a feeling of high excitement. Seeing a throng of this size, it seemed to be a trifling matter whether they were retreating or advancing. As a solemn exultation spread through his soul, even his fundamental spite against life seemed to dissolve; his lips babbled as his mind unconsciously groped for words to express his feeling: " proletariat — government by the people — armies — ours is the victory — "

But no sooner had the last sleigh vanished than Juha was beset by doubts. Before long he was nakedly afraid. The dark masses of the Paitula buildings and the rim of forest behind had quelled him; they were on the master's side, and Juha was all alone on the dark road. Even Rinne's lights twinkled coldly with an air of disclaiming any acquaintance with him. Somewhere inside those dark buildings was the gentleman. If he were now to charge out, Juha would have been powerless to stop him. Juha seemed to have become secretly endowed with the power of seeing the gentleman's thoughts at work inside the house, and at the moment he could think of nothing in the whole parish that could come up to the gentleman in importance — the gentleman and Juha, face to face.

A vague sense of grievance seized Juha as he saw the secret quick working of the master of Paitula's brains. He had the kind of gentleman's head that was always too much for you; kill him and that head would still be on his body, and the killer would only feel that he had been bested after all. It was just such gentlemen's heads — Juha seemed to see a whole row of them, as on a platform — they, and nothing else, that made the poor feel they were being made a mock of. . . . At this point Juha suddenly became aware that the firing at Kuuskoski had long ago ceased. Such a crowd had come from that direction awhile ago that there could be no one left there now. Juha was unable to picture that there might be Butchers there; no, only a dreadful emptiness that crushed and swallowed him up. And only a few yards away was the master of Paitula's head. Now, Juha realized, he was really alone; the emptiness and the gentleman's head were in league against him, they had sprung a surprise on him and were laughing. The lights at Rinne's shone lifeless.

Juha set off at a walk towards the shore, though he knew quite well that he would not dare to go away anywhere alone. He daren't even go to Rinne's; he would have to stay here until morning. Whatever was happening, he was safest here in the shadow of the house.

Again the creak of a sleigh from the shore. A solitary sleigh toiled up the bank. A sudden panic seized Juha. His recent fancies seemed to shout to him as they fled that the sleigh betokened danger for him — "It's for you it's coming!" The sleighs that had passed here earlier were far away by now. Juha was wholly in the power of the newcomers. They, too, were armed with rifles.

The sleigh turned towards the gate. Juha heard a whisper: "There the old bastard is," and the sleigh stopped. Juha's heart began to thump; his mind hastened to create a solid conviction that he had never harmed anybody, not a soul. The men stood up and one of them said shortly: "Assassination." Juha heard the word, but could make no sense of it; his knees quaked. The man repeated in a louder tone: "Assassination."

"Yes — eh, what assassin — assass — ?" stammered Juha.

"What the hell kind of a sentry are you, not knowing the password?"

But the man spoke so rapidly that Juha failed to

understand what he said. He could only take a step
towards the man and say in as ingratiating a tone as he
could muster: " Eh, what? "

" Who sent you here? " the stranger demanded.

"Rinne told me to come," Juha answered in the tone
of one answering an accusation.

" Well, stay here then and hold the horse."

The strangers were handsome men, almost gentle-
manlike in appearance. One had remarkably fine features and long and very curly hair escaping from under
his cap. He kept silent and let the others do the talking.
One of the men strode up to the house door and
knocked. Complete silence followed the sound. He
knocked again, and immediately the door swung de-
fiantly wide open. Two of the men went in, leaving the
long-haired, pretty-faced man outside. Juha would
greatly have liked to go up to him and say a friendly
word or two, a hearty comradely word, but was afraid
to do so. Best stay at the gate — he had never done
anybody any harm. Oh, he'd look faithfully after the
horse all right — they were sure to be coming out soon
— and likely as not they'd take the gentleman with
them. Juha began to feel easier in his mind — he had
never done anybody any harm.

The door swung open with a crash and the gentleman came out followed by the two men. The gentleman's movements were quick and sure, as though he
knew where he had to go; he came towards Juha, but

did not look at him. One of the two men steered the gentleman with his rifle to the driver's perch in front of the sleigh. The pretty-faced man kept a little to one side. And when the gentleman had gathered up the reins and the other two had seated themselves in the sleigh, he jumped on to the sleigh-runners behind. The party drove off down the bank in the direction from which the sleigh had come.

Juha felt such a sense of relief that he could have sat down in the snow. Nothing had happened to him, and nothing was going to happen to him. The master of Paitula had been taken away, but Juha had not been taken, but left in peace. Those fellows cursed him for not knowing the password; a good thing he hadn't known it, for that left him outside of it all. Now that the gentleman had gone, it was as though the whole house had been given into Juha's care; he felt secure and comfortable again. He would stay where he was until he saw what was going to happen — there was still no sound from Kuuskoski.

But what were they up to now down there on the shore? The sleigh had come to a halt — words, angry words, rang out and then a shot. A second shot, and then only a faint muttering. Someone was trying to soothe the startled horse. Juha's knees wobbled, his mind was a blank, but he could feel a strange, stern gentleman's head take possession of the building behind his back and breathe heavily in his direction. And beside that head, excitedly bobbing up and down, was the mistress's head. And inside Juha, in the part of him where a voice had kept on repeating only a little while ago that he had never harmed anybody, there was now silence.

The sleigh, driven at a gallop, topped the bank; in it were the three strangers. They skimmed past the house without a word. Dazed with terror and a sense of his own helplessness, Juha was turning to run after them when he heard a second sleigh approaching and a voice cry: " Stop! "

A man and a woman jumped out of the sleigh. The man came quickly towards Juha.

" Who are you? "

" I'm Johan Toivola — Rinne sent me here. I've never done anybody any harm."

" Don't jaw! Stand here and hold the horse. If any-one comes — shoot! "

The man and the woman hastened into the house by the same entrance through which the master had been brought out only a few minutes earlier. Juha would have liked to follow them in; he was terrified at being left alone, even with the horse beside him to hold. Automatically he stroked the horse's mane and adjusted its collar, but all his senses were strained outward towards the pregnant dark night. The present had fallen away from him; what was left was the being a man becomes when a flash of lightning strikes down quite close to him.

That was the night the front collapsed at Kuuskoski and the victor's forces began to pour into this parish. At one o'clock stray shots began to be heard as the victors fired on rebels who had stayed behind in the surroundings of Kuuskoski. These stragglers were the gentlest lot one could wish to meet, entirely ignorant that there had been any hostilities; they gave themselves up to the strange delusion that nothing would befall them, that in all this confusion no one would take any notice of them. That was bad for them, for few prisoners were taken at Kuuskoski. Fail to give the countersign and you were shot, and in the hurry many an innocent man may have met his death. But by then Juha Toivola was already toiling homeward along the narrow fence-side track deep in the forest. The trees on either side helped to tone down the horrors he had been through in the open village lands. This spruce-lined track had never moved with the times, but was part of the old life, and anyone who had been in a position secretly to observe the expressions in Juha's eyes as he came along this part of his road would often have had cause to smile during the course of years.

Old Juha has now definitively emerged from his revolutionary mood. The dulled rattle of rifle-shots does not engage his attention in the slightest; he is in the shelter of the forest; deeper in the woods is his wretched familiar home. And he has a strong conviction that he will have no other desire for the rest of his life than to live alone. And now that he has managed to get this far from the tight places he was in awhile ago, his life will surely henceforward proceed undisturbed. What a blessing that he has never done any harm to anybody!

While the looters were still in the main building on the Paitula estate, the first spearhead of a disorderly rabble began to show on the ice, spreading even in the dark its own raw atmosphere of despair and dejection. Only then did Juha consciously realize what was happening, and the realization set him bucking ludicrously like a sheep suddenly cut off from the flock. For the flock that now streamed towards him was not his, he had nothing in common with those people; they lacked that consciousness of security which Juha demanded of his company. The stock of his rifle began to burn his hand; the rout would soon be on him, and the two who had gone into the house might come out any minute; Rinne's lights still shone, but he would never be able to reach them and dared not even make the attempt. Danger, danger! Juha crept into a shed, stood his rifle in a dark corner, and listened to the approaching noise. Already he could distinguish voices, a child's weeping, the wailing of a woman, and on a level with these another kind of voice. Ah, no, that was his own shaky breathing; and the rifle was somewhere near like an untrustworthy being that might slip out at any moment and inform on him.

Now those two were coming out of the house and

cursing because he was not there. " Was that old devil
a Butcher? God help him, I'll give him an eternal
bread-card.

" What is going to happen to me? Lord God Father
in heaven! — What am I to say? — I didn't go to Communion last summer. I'm not going to die, not going
to die! Communion — I'll go to Communion service
as soon as ever I'm clear of this."

The murmur of voices and tramp of footsteps went
on. The voices of the two who came out of the house
died away. Were they searching for him? Good God,
if he could only partake of Holy Communion first, anything might then befall him. His legs trembled with
cold; hunger made him feel faintly sick.

Long after the noise of the rabble had died down
Juha stood in his corner. His imagination still created
moving figures where the house lay. The mistress of
Paitula seemed to be flitting about there in the company
of many angry gentlemen — of the kind that always
misunderstood you, whatever you said to them. Timidly Juha crept to the door of the shed and, seeing and
hearing nothing, was emboldened to come out into the
yard. The night was still charged with the recent happenings and seemed to be waiting for a repetition of
those scenes. The lights at Rinne's had gone out, but in
the church village, nearer Kuuskoski, lights twinkled
as though to stress that there had been no return yet
to the St. Mary's Eves of former times.

This phase with its visions of Holy Communion

passed. The rifle had remained in the shed corner, and it was only now, as his numbed thoughts began to dwell on the devious journey home still before him that Juha felt that he was indeed involved in something criminal. If he could only escape from the air of this house! He started to make his way slowly down to the ice, his ears cocked to catch the slightest sound, so that in case of need he could dash back to his rifle. He had never fired a shot in all his life, and would not fire one now; only some instinct seemed to warn him that at this moment he would be safer with a rifle if any peril threatened, and his position would be clearer. Half-way down the bank the suspicion visited his mind that this must be where they took the master of Paitula. No, he would not part from his rifle. He went back to the shed at a run, groped for his weapon, and then went more boldly down the bank.

Something black loomed in the snow where the bank and the ice met. Juha approached it, carrying his rifle; the surrounding night seemed to exhort him to do so, as though anxious on its behalf to exhibit that black object to him. Solemnity and curiosity mingled with the terror in his mind. He could see it clearly now; it lay on its back, its neck stretched backward, its chest and stomach boldly curving. Its right arm was raised as in sleep, its left flung straight out on the snow.

The master of Paitula; a little while ago he was at Rinne's and spoke those words. No thought of murder or of the murderer entered Juha's head; what he dreaded was that gentleman. He seemed to see the dead gentleman's brains on the ice in all their aggravating, overwhelming greatness.

Juha was terribly afraid and his mind instinctively sought to defend itself: " I am looking at a corpse; I suppose I can look at a corpse? Anybody who might come along would look first of all at the corpse."

Juha glanced fearfully around as though other spectators were already gathering. The dead gentleman and his brains receded again into the background. The dim night seemed to be asking him: " Dare you continue farther? You have a long way to go across open country before you can reach your own woods; once there, you are safe enough. And your rifle, where are you going to put that? "

Juha made a detour round the body and, stretching out his arm, let the rifle fall beside it as though in obedience to an unspoken order — and then ran. A shot echoed from Kuuskoski. Juha panted across the ice, off the trodden track, making for the spot where the road cut into the opposite bank. A nameless danger was at his shoulder, and all he could think of in self-defense was that he had left his rifle beside the body. He had only one aim: home, back, back to the past. The children and his dead wife flashed into his mind, a peaceful picture of a fine Sunday morning . . . all would still turn out well.

At that moment he slipped and fell; the old rupture broke out anew, his eyes watered with the pain. Two angry shots crackled from Kuuskoski way. " What have I done to you, for you to harry me like this? . . . I'm a good Social-Temocrat. . . ." Juha rested on the ice.

A new stream of fugitives pouring along the beaten track across the ice made him sit up and listen. The sound gave him so much new confidence that he was able to rise to his feet and start off again towards the road. His rifle was far behind him now. Some one would find it and for the life of him would not be able to understand how it came to be there.

At two in the morning, exhausted by his exertions, Juha reached the cabin. He had not been home for a week, and when Lempi let him in, the stuffy night smell of his house was like a welcome to him. He lit the lamp and, gazing round the room, saw the miserable little evidences of the children's unskilled attempts at house-keeping. They had obviously tried to cook themselves hot meals the best they could. The butter he had brought home from Rinne's on his last visit had not been put into the keg and covered with salt water as it should have been; its remains, stuck to the paper in which he had wrapped it, were here and there on the table in the midst of potato-skins and the remains of pickled sprats. The children huddled under their patched and torn bedclothes on their straw bed. The room was chilly; the children were not very good at fetching fuel — green, snow-covered faggots — from the forest.

This atmosphere of destitution, however, familiar throughout a lifetime, brought comfort to Juha that night. The knowledge that all that messing about in the parish was now over for good soothed his numbed heart; no need ever to go traipsing about any more. He had been — well, he had tried to be — and this was how it turned out. He would have to make a new start now.

After routing out something to eat, Juha fell asleep in the pious belief that a new life would now begin for all concerned without further ado.

And a new life did begin in the parish as soon as day had dawned. Moods and views that had been all-powerful while they lasted were suddenly swept away and entirely forgotten. From the villages farmers dressed in their best furs set out to drive to the church village, where they were to be seen standing about everywhere, in the parish hall, in the schoolhouse, in the Young People's building. If the attitude of some of them towards the recent situation had in all secrecy been more or less ambiguous, there was no doubting their whole-hearted acceptance of the new situation. Prisoners of all ages and appearances had already been brought in from various parts of the parish, and in the gray dawn a few had already paid in full for their misdeeds. Many a soft-hearted farmer was inwardly queasy at first at this rapid method of dealing out justice; the news that old so-and-so had been shot gave them a shock. But soon even the timidest had become acclimatized and were trying to outshine others in coolness. News was whispered airily, laughingly. . . .

A neutral spectator might have found it most amusing to watch those workers who had kept apart from the Revolution; there were men of this kind in cabins here and there in the parish. They had tried their best to be cautious in their speech, but for people at their stage of development the task of hiding one's true feelings is apt to be too difficult, and all too often remarks had escaped them which now troubled their consciences. Greatly silent, with eyes starting out of their heads, they tried to attract as little attention as possible. Many farmers had, it is true, let fall worse observations during the war; they had given bribes to the Reds and played the informer; but that was altogether a different matter, for it would never enter anybody's head to suspect a landowner of revolutionary sympathies. But if one happened to be a laborer and had been at all free with one's tongue, there was cause for anxiety. Such men made haste to present themselves to the conscription officers, and their wives kept discreetly out of sight. Several such women, however, were arrested and sent off north, and the rest were all the more terrified every time the shadow of a Civic Guard fell on their windows.

The murder of the master of Paitula was quickly cleared up. A rifle was discovered beside the body, and at Rinne's house, which to all appearances had been deserted in a hurry, a list of the rifles issued was found. The list showed the rifle in question to have belonged to Johan Toivola. — "So it's that old scarecrow's work." — The mistress of Paitula moreover testified to having seen Toivola at their gate on the night of the murder.

Even Juha's brain was clearer in the morning than at night. No sooner had he woke up than he grasped that all was not yet plain sailing for him. Visitors might be expected at the cabin at any time.

As he sat in the room, his glance kept falling on the door. But in that wall there was no window and he could not see the path; he found occasion to go out into the yard at very brief intervals. The cow was well supplied with hay that morning; it was groomed and the cow-house floor was thoroughly cleared of dung. Rarely had there been such activity in that quarter as today. And still no one asking for Juha.

"They'll have found the rifle by now beside the body," he thought. "Was it a good thing I left it there or bad? Anyhow it would have been worse if I had left it in the corner of the shed." But then the thought occurred to Juha that no gentleman or farmer would have done such a thing; the very idea would never have entered their heads. And now when some young gentleman found it, he'd feel puzzled and laugh, scenting in it some silly countryman's wheeze that he would never be able to fathom. Juha Toivola and a young gentleman! A more discordant, more ludicrous, more unpalatable contrast would be hard to imagine. Juha himself had been deeply aware of it all his life.

Yet life does sometimes stage such tasteless contrasts, as though intentionally making use of them to point certain hidden wordless truths. In the late afternoon two healthy-complexioned, white-toothed youths drew near to Juha's cabin, guided by the young master of Pirjola. Juha saw them from the cow-house window when they were already at the gate. He had an opportunity to study their faces unobserved, and he felt his heart stand still. They represented something new. Juha had hitherto had no clear picture of the enemy in his mind. He thought of them vaguely as sons of gentlemen and farmers, but while doing so, he saw them not as an organized whole, but as fairly negligible beings on the opposing side, as individuals of a fairly low order of brains. But these — these wore uniform caps, belts, and straps; behind them loomed the whole social order Juha had never really been able to stomach. They had got him now; best stay in the cow-house until they haled him out. He recollected: " I was on guard outside Paitula; the hay here is Pirjola's."

He heard the master of Pirjola come to the hay-shed and say: " Ay, this hay is from my farm."

" Has he robbed you of it? " one of the strangers asked in correct, stiff accents.

" I should say he has."

The other young man had meanwhile gone into the house and seen the various signs of poverty, though not with the same feelings as Juha.

" Where's your father? " he asked the girl.

" Don't know."

" Why don't you know that? "

The girl tried to think of an answer, but failed.

The stranger turned to the boy and asked him: " Do you know where your father is? "

" No."

" Has he been here today? "

" Yes."

" Well, how is it you don't know where he is now? "

The stranger spoke in a sharper tone and took a step towards the boy. The boy burst into tears.

"All right, all right, don't cry. I'm not going to eat you."

While this was going on, Juha stood pressed so close to the cow-house wall that when Pirjola opened the door all he could make out at first was the cow. Soon, however, he detected the unpleasantly familiar staring eyes of the man he sought, and anger and high spirits mingled in his tone as he shouted: " Here he is, in here! "

The man who had been in the house came hurrying up to look through the doorway. Juha saw his handsome face and the soldierlike upper part of his body and heard the clearly enunciated words: " Come out of there."

Juha made towards the door and then halted again, for his captors filled the doorway. The expression on the young soldiers' faces was that of men compelled to handle a loathsome animal.

" Well, do you hear? Come out."

Juha came out, his head trembling, his eyes starting from his head. Pirjola said, in a familiar tone because of the strangers:

" Come along now, Juha, to headquarters, though I'm not guaranteeing what's going to happen to you there."

On the way one of the soldiers asked: " Was it you who killed the master of Paitula? "

" No, it wasn't me, though I were to be shot on this very spot, no . . . nothing to do with it. . . ." Juha blew his nose agitatedly.

" And where is your rifle? "

" My rifle's there, I know . . . but I wasn't. . . ."

" You can explain all that at headquarters."

The party marched on in silence. Juha tried to calculate how much bread, sprats, wood, and hay there was at home — if Pirjola sent for his hay the cow would starve. And what was going to become of the boy? The girl would of course go into service somewhere. Hilda's fate came into his mind; tears started rolling down his cheeks. This trip could only mean death . . . he would never again come back along this fence. . . . He had never been able to finish anything all his life; he had lived with a wife, farmed a croft, been a Socialist; at bottom it had all been the same kind of thing. He had done these things because he had to do them — and now he had to die — and the children still helpless.

They too were not like other people's children, but like the work of one who doesn't rightly know how. . . .

They came to the open village lands, and Juha saw the houses in the gathering dusk as though a dozen years had passed since he last saw them. He knew clearly now that he was going to be killed; a hot wave of emotion eased the tension of his mind and caused a new gush of water from his eyes and nose. His legs were tired, but weariness was now a strange intoxication. At the back of his softened mood was an ever stronger sense of his past life, a despairing feeling of incapacity. If the sixty-year-old child of old Benjamin Nikila and his maid Maja had had a highly developed intelligence he might, on these last miles of his pilgrimage, have found a cool consolation in the circumstances of his past life. Now they merely crumbled away as it were under the flow of tears and, departing, brushed past his ever softer sensibilities.

More houses yet to be passed. Some of them teemed with soldiers — even in his private mind Juha could not think of them as Butchers. Dozens of horses were picketed in the yards. At one house a sleigh and a new escort were provided for him. He felt ever more strongly that he would never be an inhabitant of this new world. If they would only get it over quickly and not torture him. Recollections of the children and the cow stabbed at his heart — the desire to weep was now continuous. . . .

Johan Toivola's case was clear already before the trial. He had taken part in criminal activities right to the last — the latest instance was the theft of those rugs — and he had obviously played an important part in the murder of the master of Paitula, although even the keenest prosecutor, after one glance at the man, must have felt some doubt as to whether the old fellow had had any concern in the actual shooting. And there was not a single person in the whole community who felt the slightest sympathy for him. A few farmers who saw him being taken under arrest to prison were unwillingly moved to pity him. But the pity went against their grain, and once past him, they were relieved to know that they need never have anything more to do with Juha and his affairs. Their attitude was that of the man who manages to be away from home when there is slaughtering to be done, but on his return looks approvingly at the neatly cut-up meat.

Juha shivered in body and soul when he arrived at his prison quarters. He tried to assure himself that he would be shot that night; he was constantly imagining what the impact of the bullet would be like. Meanwhile his lips babbled an incoherent prayer and he had no attention left for his surroundings. The room was so tightly packed that it was impossible for all of them to lie down. A constant coughing and spitting came from every side. As the hours wore on, the expectation of death became intenser. Many prayed that God would take their lives before their fellow-men could do

2 6 4

so. The young hooligans looked ludicrous now that
gravity sat uninvited on their animal-like features. One
of them tried to engage the guard in conversation.

" You won't all be killed," remarked the guard with
a careless smile.

The night wore on, and still nobody was taken out to
be shot. Towards morning first one and then another
fell into a doze, and soon only sleepy murmurs, coughs,
and an occasional " Lord God, Heavenly Father," were
heard. Some snored; a young hooligan can sleep
soundly even in those conditions.

After dawn several new prisoners were brought into
the room. They tried to pick their way over the sleepers
to the window, but the guard forbade them and ordered
them to keep beside the wall.

" Dear is the price of blasted liberty," said one of the
newcomers.

No one got very much sleep, and all were convinced
they hadn't had a wink. Even the briefest doze, however, is a barrier between yesterday and today. In the
morning they all knew by instinct that no one was to be
shot before evening. The long day with its examina-
tions was ahead.

At half past eight the Field Judge, the Commandant,
and the local Civic Guard commander were drinking
their morning coffee. They were all in a high state of
nerves, on the point of quarreling among themselves,
for everything was still in a muddle and they had a try-

ing day before them. All kinds of things were needed, and there was nothing. The large number of prisoners was bothersome. There was no settled procedure for dealing with them. Some had been released on the guarantee of local farmers, some shot by the men on their own responsibility; the shoemakers among them had immediately been put to work. All day farmers kept on bringing in women and odd characters for examination, and a man would come, for instance, to demand a receipt for a telephone which the soldiers had taken for their own purposes. It was all so irritating that the Commandant and the Judge were constantly relapsing into Swedish, although the local commander spoke only Finnish.

The worst problem was what to do with the prisoners.

" We'll have to start off with those that will have to be shot," said the Judge.

" Oh, we don't need a trial to give every Staff hooligan his eternal bread-card," remarked the Commandant.

"Yes, but the Devil only knows which of them are Staff hooligans."

These two widely differing mental states — that of the prisoners and that of the headquarters gentlemen — come into the closest contact with each other from nine o'clock onwards. The Judge is in an energetic humor and business proceeds rapidly today. By evening forty prisoners have been sent off northward and nine are ready for execution.

Those under the death sentence are taken to a separate little building on the far side of the yard. Two soldiers with fixed bayonets and hand-grenades at their belts are set to guard them. The names of those confined in this building leak out during the day among the local soldiery. The storekeeper of the co-operative stores is one; well, you could have guessed that. Alvina Kulmala and Manda Virtanen — fancy those two women. Juha Toivola — so he's there; that means more mouths for the parish to feed.

In the little building the nine wait for night. Some of the women are passing through a phase of calmness; one asks the guard what time it is.

" Thinking of going anywhere? " the guard asks in return.

The guards are changed. Again someone asks a guard whether it isn't tiring to stand on guard.

" Thank you for asking, but we'll soon be relieved. The officer's come already."

" Is the officer going to take a turn? "

" He asked to be given the last turn."

No one felt like asking any more.

Two ignorant young human beings spent their second night of terror far away in a miserable forest shack. In the evening the girl had run all the way to the distant nearest neighbor to ask whether they had heard anything about Father. But there was no one in the house, and sobbing and panting, she jogged back through the for-

est. The boy was crying in the dark cabin, and together they prepared to endure another dreadful night.
They had always been quarreling with each other, and
Father had beaten them. But now the picture of his old
bald head and the bristling fringe below it was ever before their eyes. Their terrified weeping brought to the
surface the subconscious instincts deep down in their
blood. The simile of a captured bird and young birds
left unprotected in a nest may provoke a smile, deadly
appropriate as it is.

It was indeed an old bird that sat in the corner of
the prison building, his hands clasped around his knees,
his head nodding. He had had pains in his chest all
day and been short of breath. He had been before a
judge, but remembered nothing of what was said. Memories of events along the path of his life danced past
his consciousness. The first nights with his wife — he
was happy, after all, in those days. And then Hilda's
fate; as he now watched the successive phases of Hilda's
life since her childhood, he saw them as one continuous
journey towards the moonlit night on which she walked
into the lake. The vision was so vivid that it never
entered Juha's mind to think why it had chosen this
moment to appear to him. He only went on nodding
his head, and before long he saw the phases of his own
life as a similar consecutive journey. . . .

A low-toned voice said: " Come out." And Juha's
mind trembled back into the present and started off on

quite a different track. Such departures as this were common in the War of Independence.

The last to pass through the cemetery gate was Juha Toivola. The others, younger in years, hastened on almost at a run; only the pot-bellied storekeeper lagged behind to keep Juha company.

Cold, hunger, and lack of sleep have done old Juha good. The pain in his chest has gone and he can breathe now without difficulty; at least he is less aware of bodily discomfort. His trembling, too, has become unconscious and his thoughts are as though held together within a ring which remains motionless all the while thousands upon thousands of tiny sensations fiercely jostle one another. This goes on as long as anything continuous is happening, as when the party marches on without new orders. But as soon as anything special happens, however slight, as when the officer pushes the iron gate wider open, or when he turns to look behind and the barrel of his rifle swings in the darkness, a pang of weary despair shoots through Juha. Not a piercing pang, but rather as though someone were striking at his vitals with a leather ball.

The long line of graves dug in the sand comes into sight. " Halt! " The front ranks stop, but those behind still take a few steps. Then they stand at ease, breathing audibly; one of the prisoners collapses to his hands and knees, but no one says anything. The ring around

Juha's thoughts has vanished; he is drawn irresistibly to the ground, but manages to stand. He begins to have the same feeling as once after he had partaken of Holy Communion when he was ill. And isn't it a fact that he has been quite recently to Communion? He remembers plainly standing in the corner of the shed at Paitula in the happy past, but after that everything is a blank. Justice and injustice, guilt and innocence, are questions altogether alien to this situation, to this state of mind. They have no place even on the farthest outskirts of his consciousness. "What dress was Hilda wearing when she left home, in the sunshine? Yes, that was it, and those were the boots she wore."

Juha's senses register what is happening. The potbellied storekeeper has been fetched without a word from behind the others, told to take off his shoes and clothes; he is doing that now. Now he steps down into the grave; the sand yields a little under his feet. An angry suspense — rac nic-nac rac tr-rac — the breechlocks rattle. A long, long silence, during which the crushing sense of something unnatural happening reaches a climax. The crash of fire is a tremendous relief. After the first execution is over, everything proceeds easier.

The next man is ordered to undress, step down into the grave —·and so on. The shots crash out, trying in vain to arouse benumbed minds. Apparently there is to be no hero in this batch. The women keep up a tremulous noise that is not weeping, but probably the earliest primitive squealing of the dam parted from its cubs. Their unavailing prayers and kneelings are long ago over.

It happened that our old unsavory friend Juha was last. He was still so far conscious as to notice this and derive a kind of dull emotion from the fact. He was also quite convinced that he had just partaken of Holy Communion; he mumbled ceaselessly to himself: " Lord Jesus take my spirit." He hesitated a little before taking off his trousers, for his drawers were very ragged (a slipshod fellow like him would naturally have neglected to replenish his wardrobe from the Red Guard stores) and also, as a result of what he had gone through, a little — Nevertheless he opened his belt and slipped out of his trousers. " Lord Jesus take my spirit, Lord Jesus take my spirit."

At the bottom of the grave a fairly large pool of blood had collected when Juha stepped down into it in his tattered socks. A grateful languor led him unwittingly to lay himself down on the pile of corpses. The edges of the grave showed dark against the faintly glowing sky. Then a shudder robbed his languor of its charm. A clenched fist pressed uncomfortably on the back of his neck.

For a second he has forgotten what is before him, but the next minute the commanding voice of the officer bids him get to his feet. In moments of stress men instinctively obey an order. Juha struggles painfully to his feet, and holding up his ragged undergarments, Juha Toivola is blown into the mighty all-embracing state of being known as death without a " last thought " of any kind.

His sufferings, which surely help in an invisible ledger to swell the credit account of the people of whose collective entity he knew nothing, were longer and greater than those of many — perhaps of any — on whom so much pity is expended.

The officer and his men already march far away from the graveyard. The life of Johan Toivola has reached its natural end; there remains only the usual valediction. But it is hard to find anything weighty enough for that purpose, for Juha met his death while the storm raged over Finland at its worst and the rest of mankind was still passionately trying to guess what the happiness was that it was straining with so much labor to achieve. Were one gifted with second sight, one might perhaps learn something if on this dim night one were to steal to the graveyard, descend into the grave beside the pool of blood and the pile of corpses, and there listen to the silence.

It is by no means certain that one's dominating sensation would be horror. Spring hovers already in the graveyard trees and in the air, promising once again bird-song and the scent of flowers and to the growing generation days full of bliss. Ever nearer they advance towards that happiness, the definition of which has occupied mankind for centuries. Today they still believe that the physical body and its demands, the community, and other such matters are in the closest connection with that happiness. But granted that conceptions still move on this low plane, time is long. And already we have come so far that most people, at the moment of their death, do experience a flash of it; it is precisely that which gives a nocturnal graveyard such a homogeneous atmosphere, once we have grasped this circumstance. And some day, as the existence of mankind continues, it will yet spread into the kingdom of the living.

A NOTE ON THE TYPE

THIS BOOK is set on the Linotype in Baskerville.
The punches for this face were cut under the super-
vision of George W. Jones, the eminent English
printer and the designer of Granjon and Estienne.
Linotype Baskerville is a facsimile cutting from
type cast from the original matrices of a face de-
signed by John Baskerville, a writing-master of Bir-
mingham, for his own private press. The original
face was the forerunner of the " modern " group of
type faces, known today as Scotch, Bodoni, etc.
After his death in 1775, Baskerville's punches and
matrices were sold in France and were used to produce the sumptuous Kehl edition of Voltaire's
works.

This book was composed, printed, and bound by
The Plimpton Press, Norwood, Mass. The paper
was made by S. D. Warren Co., Boston. The typog-
raphy and designs are based on originals by W. A.
Dwiggins.